"Look, this isn't some sort of test."

A grim look came into Bryce's eyes as he spoke. "You're flying tomorrow, but a couple of drinks now won't affect you."

"All right. I'll have a gin and tonic, please," Leigh acquiesced.

When the drinks came Bryce lifted his and said, "Cheers," then touched his glass to hers. Their eyes met and held over the clinking glasses, and Leigh hastily took a long drink. She wondered why he had asked her to such a posh place.

It certainly wasn't out of the goodness of his heart, she decided cynically. And it wasn't to acquaint himself with one of his employees because he'd made it quite clear that he didn't intend her to stay one for long. So...why?

SALLY WENTWORTH

flying high

Harlequin Books

TORONTO · NEW YORK · LOS ANGELES · LONDON
AMSTERDAM · PARIS · SYDNEY · HAMBURG
STOCKHOLM · ATHENS · TOKYO · MILAN

Harlequin Presents first edition March 1983
ISBN 0-373-10581-9

Original hardcover edition published in 1982
by Mills & Boon Limited

CHAPTER ONE

THE building that housed Allerton Air Charters
was more imposing than Leigh had expected it to
be. It was situated on the western side of the airport, with its back to the runway, and stood out
from the conglomeration of other buildings around
it because of its smart, modern appearance; all
large windows and pre-fabricated concrete. It was
L-shaped and two-storeyed, with a neatly laid out
car park within the area formed by the two wings.
Leigh drove on past some warehouses, the local
flying club and a repair shop, and parked in front
of the Allerton building in a space marked
'Visitors'.

A brief glance at her watch confirmed that she
still had over twenty minutes before her appointment, as she'd planned. Unhurriedly, she got out
of the Mini and took a good look around the airport. It wasn't very large as airports go, had only
really started to be used commercially in the last
ten years, since the large new town of Shepton
Ferrers had been built in the vicinity. Now its main
runway had been lengthened to take commercial
aircraft, and there was a whole row of hangars
together with the smaller offices and repair shops
that went with them.

Leigh locked the Mini and strolled round to the
back of the Allerton building. Here double doors
opened directly on to the tarmac so that passengers

only had a short walk to the aircraft. There were only two planes painted in the distinctive Allerton turquoise and white colours standing on the tarmac at the moment, a twin-engined Piper Aztec which was obviously used for air-taxi work, and a smaller Arrow. Over on the left there were two large hangars with the Allerton name high up over the doors, one of which was open to show another aircraft in the process of being serviced, but Leigh walked over to the two parked planes, looking them over closely. They were both well maintained, the paintwork unchipped and sparkling, the windscreens clean, and the tyres looked good. The Aztec was by far the newer of the two planes, but the Arrow was in excellent condition, even when she crouched down to look at the undercarriage Leigh could see no telltale streaks of oil or rust. Straightening up, she peered in at the windows, trying to see if the plane was as clean inside as it was out.

'If you're looking for the flying school, you've come to the wrong place.'

The harsh voice behind her made her jump, and Leigh turned quickly to see a tall, broad-shouldered man in mechanic's overalls striding across the tarmac towards her from the direction of the open hangar. He was frowning and didn't look at all pleased to see her, but Leigh was quite pleased to see him; it showed that Allerton's security was good and they didn't let strangers go poking around their aircraft. The man came close enough to see her properly and his eyes ran over her tall, boyishly-slim figure not unappreciatively, then his eyes came up and stayed there as he took in her heart-shaped face with straight nose and high

cheekbones, finely arched eyebrows over green
eyes, and the richness of her medium length chestnut hair.

He stopped a couple of yards away and Leigh
moved away from the plane, murmuring an
apology and giving the man a spontaneous smile.
It wasn't reciprocated. His mouth merely curved sardonically as he pointed back the way she'd come.

'The clubhouse for the flying school is back there
and about a hundred yards along to the right. You
can't miss it,' he told her pointedly.

'Thanks, but I'm not interested in flying lessons,'
Leigh answered. 'I was just taking a look at the
planes because . . .'

He cut her off abruptly. 'Because you were
hoping for a free ride, I suppose.'

Leigh laughed. 'Do you get many people hanging
around, hoping for a joyride?'

'Enough. Young boys mostly, and those we
chase away.'

The man had hard grey eyes; Leigh found herself
held by them and felt compelled to say, 'And the
girls?'

His rather thin lips drew into a definite sneer
and his eyes ran over her again, but this time
mentally undressing her. 'Oh, sometimes they get
what they want, but they usually end up by paying
for it—one way or another.'

Leigh flushed and her eyes grew cold. Impossible
not to understand what he meant and to resent his
attitude. Obviously a wolf in mechanic's clothing.
And a downright chauvinist one at that! Which
was a shame, because her first, instantaneous impression of him had been favourable: she'd liked

his even-featured, dark-haired handsomeness and
crisp air of authority. It was also a shame because
if, as she guessed, he was the chief mechanic at
Allerton's, it would mean that their paths would
often cross once she started to work there, which
might prove to be awkward. Leigh sighed and went
to walk past him, but the man moved in front of
her.

'Of course I might be able to arrange something
for you if you're willing to . . .'

'Thanks,' Leigh cut in shortly, 'but I'm fussy
who I fly with.'

'Suit yourself,' he said insolently.

'Oh, don't worry—I will.' With heightened
patches of colour in her cheeks, Leigh stepped
round him and walked quickly back the way she'd
come, conscious that the horrible man was standing and watching her. When she got back to her
car, she saw that there was still over five minutes
left, so she sat in the Mini and combed her hair,
which had become a little windswept from the light
breeze which had blown across the open plain of
the tarmac. She also checked her lipstick in the
vanity mirror and made sure the collar of her cream
blouse sat properly on the jacket of the brown
tweed suit she was wearing. Picking up the case
containing all her certificates and licences, she
checked the time once more, saw that there was
only one minute to go, and again got out of the
car. This time she walked up to the front of the
Allerton building and in through the main door.

Inside there was the usual modern reception area
with brown leather tubular chairs, a coffee table
with copies of *Flight* on it, and several large potted

plants. The girl behind the reception desk was as clinically modern and smart as the room, with blonde hair cut in a neat, fringed bell shape, and a very curvy figure in a close-fitting sweater and straight skirt. The girl looked up from the typewriter she was using when Leigh came in, gave a practised smile and said, 'Can I help you?'

'I have an appointment to see Mr Bryce Allerton. My name is Leigh Bishop.'

A slight frown creased the girl's forehead, but she said politely, 'Would you take a seat, please? I'll tell Mr Allerton you're here.'

Leigh obediently sat in one of the brown leather chairs and picked up a magazine. It was only last month's and one she hadn't read, but she gazed at it unseeingly, her thoughts going back to the rather nasty little encounter on the tarmac, but then she determinedly pushed it to the back of her mind. It was a nuisance, nothing more. She had had far worse to deal with in the past and would probably have to do so again in the future. There was no point in worrying about it. All she must think of at the moment was meeting her new boss, the head of Allerton Air Charters. But she was given little chance to do so because the receptionist, after speaking on the internal phone for a few seconds, nodded to her and said, 'Would you go up to Mr Allerton's office now, please? It's up the stairs and the first door on the right.'

'Thank you.' Leigh went in the direction indicated, feeling rather nervous, although she shouldn't have been; after all, it wasn't as if she was going to be interviewed for a job—she'd already got it. After her last job had folded she had gone to an agency and they had given her name to Allerton's. After that everything had been conducted by letter as Leigh lived so far away and Allerton's were, from what Leigh had gathered, in a hurry to replace someone. So, after a minimum of delay in which they had checked her qualifications, Allerton's had engaged her, again by letter. Today was just a formality really, to sign her contract of employment and introduce herself, but even so she still felt slightly nervous.

A somewhat muffled voice called out for her to come in when she knocked on Mr Allerton's door. Leigh pushed it open and found herself in a businesslike office lit by a window overlooking the tarmac and runways. Predominating the room was a large desk with two telephones on it as well as several work trays, and against the wall there were a couple of filing cabinets. That the room was also used for customers, though, was proved by the carpet on the floor, the two comfortable-looking chairs opposite the desk and a drinks cabinet over in the corner. The room, at the moment, was empty, but the same voice called out to her from the open door of a cloakroom where the occupant was obviously washing his hands. 'Take a seat. I'll be with you in a moment.'

Leigh did so and took a good look at the desk. Everything on it was neatly arranged; the pens and pencils in their tray, the points of the pencils sharpened, the blotting paper in the pad was new and unmarked and the papers in the trays neatly aligned, not just thrown in anyhow. Leigh sat back satisfied; she believed that you could tell a lot about

a man's character from his desk, and this one's
neatness pleased her. From its exact arrangement
she guessed that Mr Allerton was, or had once
been, a pilot himself. Perhaps he'd learnt to fly in
the war and had started the firm immediately afterwards—a lot of air charter firms had come into
being then, although a great many of them hadn't
survived, especially since the latest recession. The
door of the cloakroom closed and she looked up,
expecting to see a man in his sixties. She didn't;
she found herself looking into the cold grey eyes of
a man who couldn't have been more than thirty-
five at the most. And she'd seen those eyes before—
on the mechanic she'd had the brush with out on
the tarmac!

The grey eyes widened incredulously and then
grew angry. 'How the hell did you find your way
in here?' Leigh opened her mouth to reply but he
swept on, 'Look, I don't know what you hope to
gain by coming here, but this is neither the time
nor the place. Right now I have an appointment
with a new pilot.'

Surprise had brought Leigh to her feet. It took a
few seconds to adjust to the fact that the man was
the boss and not just a mechanic, and then a new
shock wave hit her. It must have occurred to him
at exactly the same moment, because she saw en-
lightenment start to dawn even before she said,
'Yes, I know. I'm the pilot.'

He stared at her, still not quite believing it, perhaps not wanting to believe it, then he said harshly,
'The pilot I hired was named Leigh Bishop.'

'Yes, that's my name.'

Leigh groaned inwardly, knowing exactly what

he was going to say next. He'd thought she was a man! It had happened to her two or three times in the past owing to her unusual Christian name that could be used by either sex. But it honestly hadn't occurred to her that it had happened again; they had checked her records, surely somewhere they had mentioned her sex. But if they had he obviously hadn't noticed it.

'Leigh is a man's name,' Bryce Allerton pointed out grimly.

'But it can be given to girls, too.' Trying to make the best of it, Leigh held out her hand. 'How do you do, Mr Allerton?'

He looked at her stonily for a moment before moving a couple of paces towards her and reluctantly shaking hands. His grip was strong, firm and decisive, a token of the man's physical strength. Going round to the other side of the desk, he gestured to her to sit down before doing so himself.

He showed no inclination to open proceedings, merely looking at her broodingly, so Leigh picked up her documents case and said brightly, 'I've brought along all my licences and certificates. I had my last medical check just two months ago and was passed A1. I also . . .'

Bryce Allerton, his voice heavy with sarcasm, interrupted her. 'I don't doubt your qualifications, *Miss* Bishop,' he said, emphasising the title. 'I've already had them checked. Tell me,' he added sardonically, 'do you usually resort to this kind of trickery when you're applying for a job?'

Leigh's mouth tightened. 'Trickery?'

'Letting your prospective employer believe that

you're a man,' he explained with deliberate insolence.

'I did no such thing,' Leigh retorted. 'You could easily have checked if you'd been in any doubt.'

'I wasn't; it never occurred to me that you might be a woman. Just as, I suppose, it didn't occur to you to add Miss after your name when you signed your letters.' He looked at her ringless left hand. 'It is Miss, I take it?'

'Yes, it is,' Leigh confirmed, adding tartly, 'And I didn't notice you putting Mr after your signature either.'

'It's never been necessary; no one's ever been in any doubt about *my* gender. And I certainly wouldn't stoop to using a cheap subterfuge to get a job,' he added sharply.

Leigh's temper rose, but she fought to control it. Bryce Allerton was looking at her contemptuously, dislike plain in his face, and she guessed that he was deliberately trying to rile her so that she would get angry enough to tell him what to do with his job and walk out. Maybe a couple of years ago pride would have made her do just that, but she needed this job, needed it badly, so she said in as reasonable a tone as she could manage, 'Look, Mr Allerton, I'm sorry if there's been a misunderstanding, but I assure you that it wasn't deliberate. Really it wasn't. There are a lot of women pilots now and more coming along all the time. And anyway, I have all the necessary qualifications for the job; I'm sure you wouldn't have agreed to employ me if they hadn't been good enough.'

She looked at him hopefully, but he was still regarding her with implacable coldness. Roughly, he said, 'Air charter flying is damned hard work, Miss Bishop. It isn't pleasant little hops round the country to a fixed timetable with everyone else doing the organising and back-up work. We fly at unsociable hours in all weathers, and I expect the pilots to turn to and help with other work whenever it's necessary, and that includes loading and unloading.' His eyes ran disparagingly down her slim figure, a far cry from the way he'd looked at her out on the tarmac. 'I doubt if you've even got the strength to lift your own suitcase.'

Leigh flushed and gripped her hands together in her lap. 'I'm much stronger than I look. And I'm not afraid of hard work, Mr Allerton. As you'll find out when I start flying for you,' she added deliberately, deciding to force the issue.

His left eyebrow rose cynically. '*When* you start flying for me?'

Speaking as calmly as she could, Leigh answered, 'I have your letter accepting my application and stating the terms of employment. You have mine accepting them.'

He got to his feet abruptly and stood glowering down at her. Then he put his hands on the desk and leaned forward, looming over her menacingly. 'Very well, Miss Bishop, if we're going to speak plainly, then I'll tell you that no way do I want a woman pilot working for me. I have enough problems among my work force as it is without adding another source of trouble.'

'But what makes you think I'd cause trouble?' Leigh protested.

He laughed harshly. 'A young, attractive girl, available, with the added glamour of being a pilot—you'd be nothing but trouble wherever you wiggled that pretty little bottom of yours,' he replied with deliberate insolence.

Leigh felt her colour heightening and strove to control herself, her nails digging into her palms. At length she said icily, 'It's hardly my fault if you're unable to control your workers, Mr Allerton,' and had the satisfaction of seeing him frown in anger at the thrust. Then she went on, 'And if we're going to speak frankly, then may I remind you of the Sex Discrimination Act? You have accepted my application on the basis of my experience and qualifications. The only reason you've given for wanting to change your mind is because I'm a woman. I would say that made a perfect example of discrimination to place before an industrial tribunal, wouldn't you? You'd probably incur a great deal of legal costs and end up having to employ me anyway.'

He stared at her, his expression glacial. 'Are you threatening me, Miss Bishop?'

'No,' Leigh answered steadily, 'I'm just stating a fact. Because that's what *will* happen if you throw me out of here.'

Bryce Allerton straightened up, glared at her for a long moment and then sat down again. 'How old are you?' he demanded suddenly.

'I'm twenty-five.'

'And how long have you been flying?'

'I took my first solo flight on my seventeenth birthday,' Leigh answered. 'I got my private pilot's licence a few weeks later and I added all the ratings for night flying, instructing and that sort of thing as soon as I could, and then took my commercial licence when I was twenty-one. I've been earning my living by flying ever since.'

'In short, a flying fanatic,' he said with sardonic contempt.

Leigh bit her lip. 'If you like. I only know that from my first lesson I've never wanted to do anything else.'

He looked at her with a thoughtful frown, then drew a folder towards him and opened it. Leigh recognised her own letter on top of the small pile of papers inside. He pushed it aside to look at her flying record and said, 'This firm you were with before, South-East Air, how long were you with them?'

'Four years. Ever since I got my commercial licence.'

He glanced at her curriculum vitae. 'And you were flying in the co-pilot's seat on Islanders and Trislanders on scheduled flights?'

'Yes.'

'Quite a comedown, then, to fly charters,' he remarked contemptuously.

Leigh ignored the gibe, merely saying, 'I'm licensed to fly any plane you have here, Mr Allerton. And in any conditions.'

He frowned. 'Why did you leave South-East Air?'

'I didn't. It folded. There were just too many third-level airlines trying to grab a share of the market, taking Eurocrats across to Brussels and Paris, that kind of run. And South-East couldn't compete, especially when they lost a lucrative concession to a bigger airline.' But he must already know all this, Leigh decided as she gave him the

explanation. Everyone in the air world would
be well aware of the troubles that had hit the air
passenger industry over the last few years of recession.

He held out a hand. 'Let me see your licences.'

Silently Leigh passed him the little pile of documents that represented her whole working life and
the dearly won fulfilment of most of her ambitions.
That her record was good, she knew; she'd had to
be good to win and keep a place in a hard-hit industry. She was intensely proud of the fact that
there had never once, in all her years of flying,
been a black mark against her. All that was left
now was the big jet airliners owned by international
first level airlines, and helicopters, but Leigh was
realistic enough to know that with so many good
male pilots looking for jobs, she stood little chance
of ever attaining these ambitions.

Bryce Allerton looked over her licences carefully,
probably trying to find some fault, Leigh thought
bitterly. She had the opportunity to look at him
more closely now and note the hard, determined
line of his jaw, with no hint of softness in his eyes
or of humour around his mouth. He looked like a
man who didn't suffer fools gladly, who knew what
he wanted and went ahead and took it. Looking
up, he caught her watching him. For a second their
glances met, but then he disparagingly tossed her
documents back to her. Leigh picked them up from
the desk and put them carefully back in her case,
willing herself to keep calm, not to let him get
to her. Placing the bag on the floor by the chair,
she sat back, folded her hands in her lap and
looked at her prospective employer expectantly.

No way was she going to make the next move.

They faced each other out for a few moments and then Bryce Allerton smiled sardonically and got to his feet. 'All right, Miss Bishop, we both know there's really only one way to tell how good a pilot you are, isn't there?'

Leigh looked up at him and her heart sank, despite herself. 'You want me to take you up,' she said flatly.

'Just that. Let's go, shall we?'

'Very well.'

He held the door open for her in exaggerated chivalry and then led her down the stairs and through a door marked 'AIR CREW ONLY' which opened into a comfortable-looking lounge where two men were sitting at a table, drinking mugs of coffee and writing up reports. They looked up curiously as Leigh and Bryce Allerton entered, their expressions becoming astonished when they saw that the boss had a girl with him, and when they noted the grim look on his face. Allerton gave the men a brief nod but didn't attempt to introduce Leigh to them, just motioned her to a glazed door that led out on to the tarmac. Then he hesitated. 'Just a moment; I'd better tell my secretary where I'll be.'

He was back within five minutes.

'We'll take the Arrow,' he informed her briefly.

Crossing to the plane, he opened the door and stood aside so that she could get into the left-hand seat, but Leigh wasn't going to fall for that one. She put her bag in the plane but then started going round it doing a pre-flight external check, and doing it extra carefully.

'I thought you looked over the plane earlier,' Bryce Allerton remarked.

'I didn't know I was going to fly it then. I just wanted to see what kind of airline I was joining.'

His eyes narrowed, but he merely said, 'It's perfectly okay; my mechanics checked it this morning.'

Leigh raised her head from where she had been checking the air intakes to the engine and looked at him coldly, knowing the game he was playing. No self-respecting pilot would take someone else's word that a plane was ready for take-off, they always checked for themselves. 'Thank you, but I prefer to do my own inspection,' she informed him.

He shrugged and leaned against the fuselage, whistling tunelessly. Leigh gritted her teeth but carried on, making sure she left nothing out, because she was quite certain that although Bryce Allerton appeared to be quite unconcerned and hardly seemed to be watching her, he was noting every move she made. At length she was satisfied and climbed up into the plane, stepping down into the cockpit and moving into the pilot's seat on the left, glad that she'd worn a full, pleated skirt so that she hadn't given too much of a leg show as she'd climbed up the walkway on the starboard wing roof.

Bryce Allerton climbed in beside her and closed the door, reaching up to twist the top clip above his head into the 'Locked' position. He was very broad, taking up more than his fair share of the seating space, and somehow his obvious dislike of her seemed deeper and more menacing in the

confined space of the cabin. Ignoring him as far as
it was possible to ignore someone who was watching her like a hawk, Leigh picked up the plane's
maintenance card and saw that the date on it was
only three days old, so that was okay. Then she
went carefully through the pre-start checks, her
hands moving efficiently across the controls: mixture, throttle, prop, boost, pump . . . When she'd
finished, she twisted the key to start the engine and
it burst sweetly into life, the propeller turning so
fast that it became invisible. Leigh throttled back
to a thousand revs per minute, put on her headset,
then called the control tower and asked for taxi
clearance.

'Good morning, Shepton Tower; this is Delta
Lima Hotel Whisky Bravo, pre-flight check and
request taxi.'

The air controller's voice came tinnily back
through the headset. 'Good morning, Whisky
Bravo, clear taxi runway two-five. QNH one-zero-
one-four, QFE one-zero-zero-five, wind two-three-
zero at one-two.'

Calmly Leigh noted the information on the clipboard and acknowledged. Reaching down, she
released the parking brake and eased the Arrow
forward on to the taxi-way, yawing the plane
gently to right and then left as she went to check
the movement of the turn needle and the com-
passes. It was some time since she had flown an
Arrow, perhaps as much as a couple of years, and
at first it felt strange and awkward after the larger
planes she had been used to, but the feel of it soon
came back and by the end of the taxi-way she con-
fidently ran up the engine and checked the propel-

ler and magnetos. Then she went through the pre-take-off checks, once more going over all the controls and dials, making doubly sure that all was working perfectly. Control gave her clearance to take off and Leigh pulled out on to the runway. She glanced once at her passenger, found him watching her intently, then determinedly gave her full attention to the task ahead as she accelerated down the runway and lifted the Arrow gracefully into the air.

Immediately the wheels left the ground Leigh experienced the exhilarating feeling she always got whenever she had a plane under her hands. Being a passenger was never quite the same, even in a small craft such as this; it was being able to handle the plane that gave that tremendous surge to the spirits, made her feel as if she was literally on top of the world. At a thousand feet, with the wheels and flaps up she reduced power to the en-route climb setting up to four thousand feet. Now that she was in the air all her nervousness had gone; she was in an element she knew and could handle. Unlike the man sitting so watchfully beside her; Leigh had an idea that she'd never be able to handle him in a million years. She wondered whether he was married; if so his wife must have a tough time of it if his attitude towards herself was anything to go by. But perhaps he was different at home. Perhaps he had just been nasty to her because he thought that she'd made a fool of him through the mix-up over her name. No man liked to be made a fool of or to be shown up, especially by a young, attractive girl; Leigh had found that out the hard way quite some time ago when she had gained a rating for her licence that a boy-friend had failed, and he had promptly dropped her like the proverbial hot cake, dating instead a very pretty but empty-headed girl who didn't know port from starboard. No, in Leigh's experience men definitely didn't like girls who were too clever and could outsmart them.

At four thousand feet she levelled out and adjusted the pitch of the propeller and settled the speed at a hundred and fifty miles an hour. She glanced towards Bryce Allerton, waiting for him to tell her what he wanted her to do, but noticed that her skirt had slipped up a little and was showing her knees. Automatically she took a hand off the control wheel to pull it down and found that he was watching her, his lip curled in sardonic mockery. Leigh remembered, then, the way he had behaved when she had first met him on the tarmac back at Shepton, and decided that he probably wasn't married after all—married men didn't usually act like that, and besides, no woman in her right mind would want him!

'When did you last fly one of these?' he demanded.

Leigh took off the headset and switched over to the cabin speaker. 'About two years ago.'

'Think you can take her out of a spin?'

'Yes,' she answered levelly.

'Go ahead, then.'

Leigh had been expecting something like this; there wouldn't have been much point in his bringing her up here unless he was going to put her to some sort of test. She climbed to get enough height and then put the aircraft into a spin, handling it with

calm self-assurance, going through the recovery
drill and always in complete control. He made no
comment afterwards, just put her through a whole
load more simulated emergencies and tests, really
piling it on. Leigh had had examiners sitting beside
her before, many times, but never once had she
been put through a test as exacting as this.

After about half an hour of it, Bryce Allerton
said, 'Okay, she's all yours.' Adding, 'Throw her
about a bit if you want.'

Leigh looked at him sharply, surprised that he
had made the offer; perhaps the way she had
handled the plane had made a good impression and
convinced him that she was a capable pilot, after
all. Her eyes lit up; she would enjoy a chance for
some free flying. She was about to say so and put
the Arrow into a barrel roll, when something—
perhaps some tension in his silence, perhaps just
intuition—made her realise that it was a trap to
catch her out. So she merely said, 'Thanks, but I'll
head back to Shepton aerodrome now, if it's all
right with you?'

He gave a brief nod, and she had the satisfaction
of seeing a flicker of annoyance in his face. Leigh
gave an inward sigh of relief, grateful that she
hadn't yielded to temptation; this was neither the
time nor the place to practise stunt flying! Putting
on the headset effectively put an end to any further
conversation with Bryce Allerton, and she concen-
trated instead on calling up the control tower for
permission to land, going steadily through the pre-
landing check list, sure that he wasn't relaxing his
vigilance for one second.

Shepton came into sight again within minutes

and Leigh banked to turn in line with the runway.
She could see the orange windsock blowing almost
at right angles to the runway and allowed for the
crosswind during her slow descent. The Arrow
touched down on the tarmac, the two people inside
the cabin hardly feeling the impact of the undercarriage on the ground, so lightly did Leigh bring
it down. At the end of the runway, she wheeled the
plane round in a circle and taxied back to the
Allerton hangars, placing the plane back in exactly
the same position as she had found it. After signing
off with the control tower, she unhurriedly completed writing up the flight in the plane's log book
before turning to look at Bryce Allerton again.

She had expected him to be waiting impatiently
for her to finish, but was surprised to find that he
was looking rather abstractedly out of the window.
He turned, saw that she was ready, and said
abruptly, 'Let's go to my office.'

He didn't offer to help her down, just strode on
ahead with Leigh hurrying after him, wondering
what was coming. They went back the way they'd
come, through the crew room. There was another
man there now and they all three moved hurriedly
away as Bryce Allerton pushed open the door, so
that Leigh was embarrassingly aware that they'd
been watching her as she'd flown in. But at least
she had the comfort of knowing she had made a
decent landing. Their curiosity was quite open now,
but Leigh had no time to give the men more than a
brief glance before Bryce Allerton had walked
through the room into the corridor beyond and
she had to go after him.

In his office, he strode behind the desk, then

turned to look at her. Leigh, slightly out of breath, closed the door and turned to face him. His features were quite implacable, there was no sign of mollification, or that his attitude towards her had softened by even one iota. She knew, suddenly but surely, that no matter how brilliantly she had piloted the Arrow, nothing would have made any difference to him. Slowly she moved forward into the room and waited for him to speak.

Thrusting his hands into his trouser pockets, he said curtly, 'Do you still want to work for me, knowing that I don't want to take you on?'

'Yes,' Leigh answered boldly.

'All right; I'll admit that I don't want the hassle of going before some damn discrimination board.'

'Or the publicity either, I should imagine,' Leigh cut in.

'Or that,' he agreed, his eyes flickering over her in open distaste. 'So it seems that I have no choice but to employ you on the terms we agreed.' Sitting down, he opened her folder again and tossed a paper over to her side of the desk. 'Here's your contract of employment for you to sign. When can you start?'

'Almost immediately,' Leigh replied as she crossed to the desk and took the pen he was holding out to her. 'I've brought most of my things with me and I just have to find somewhere to stay.' She was trying to read the contract as she spoke, her eyes quickly running down the page. It seemed all right, the salary, holiday conditions etc. were the same as they'd agreed by letter.

'You haven't got anything lined up?'

'No. I thought I'd stay in a hotel until I can get something more permanent fixed up.'

'There's a small hotel on the outskirts of the town: they should have a room available. The receptionist will phone them for you later. I'd like you to start tomorrow, if that's convenient?'

'Yes, that's fine.' Leigh had turned the contract over and was hastily trying to read the other side, but Bryce Allerton was impatiently holding his hand out for it. Leigh signed her name, dated the document and handed it back.

A glint of satisfaction showed in her new boss's eyes for a second as he took it from her. His tone had been quite conciliatory during the last few minutes, but now it became instantly curt again.

'I want you here at six tomorrow morning to fly down to Brighton and pick up a cargo of French vegetables and fly them up to Scotland, then return with another cargo to Stansted before coming back here. Do you see any problems in that?'

'No, I don't think so,' Leigh answered. 'Have I got to be ready to take off at six? Do you want me to file my flight plan before then?'

'If it wouldn't be too much trouble,' he drawled insolently. 'Of course, if you're the type that prefers a nine-to-five job we can always tear this up,' he added, pointing to the contract.

'That won't be necessary. I can be here at whatever time you specify, so long as you make it clear exactly what time you *do* mean,' Leigh stressed, her anger rising again.

Bryce Allerton looked at her derisively but didn't labour the point. Picking up the internal phone on his desk, he said into the receiver, 'Carol, get on to that hotel near the station—the Beechwood, that's right. Ask them if they have a room vacant and, if they have, book it for Miss Bishop on a weekly basis.'

He put down the receiver and stood up briskly, glancing at his watch. 'I've just time to take you down to introduce you to our chief mechanic and one or two others.'

For a second time Leigh followed him down to the crew room, feeling slightly puzzled. The anger and annoyance seemed to have left him and he had spoken in a lighter, more normal tone. Perhaps he had decided that if there was no help for it, then he would have to make the best of employing her. She certainly hoped so; because she couldn't see any joy in working for a man who was actively against her. If she hadn't needed this job so badly, she would never even have considered it.

The three men who had been there previously were all still in the crew room and looked up immediately when they walked in. Leigh stood rather diffidently in the doorway, but Bryce Allerton arrogantly motioned her forward and introduced her to the nearest man. He was about fifty, his hair just starting to turn grey, with a wealth of experience in his eyes.

'This is Don Chapman, who works for us part time. He used to be with B.A.'

All the men had got to their feet and Leigh shook hands with each in turn.

'This is our chief mechanic, Vic Parker.' Another middle-aged man with a surprised but not unfriendly smile.

'And this is one of our other pilots, Mike Stewart,' Bryce Allerton finished. A younger man this, about thirty, who looked her over with intrigued, speculative interest.

In fact all their faces were alive with expectant interest as they looked at the boss. He waited for a few seconds, seeming to Leigh to be deliberately drawing out the suspense, before he introduced her in turn. 'This,' he said coldly, 'is Miss Leigh Bishop, who's joining us as a pilot. But you don't have to worry,' he added scathingly, 'her appointment is a very temporary one. She won't be with us very long.'

Her first reaction was to turn on him and demand to know what the hell he was talking about; she'd just signed a contract of employment, hadn't she? But somehow Leigh managed to control herself in front of the other men. But the fact that Bryce Allerton had chosen to make such an announcement when they weren't alone and she couldn't tackle him about it only served to increase her anger and indignation. But Mike Stewart was saying something and she had to give him her attention.

'Welcome to Allerton's. I must say you're a great improvement on the last pilot we had. Isn't she, Bryce?' He turned, his face alight with amused mockery and speculation, to his employer, but received only a stony look in return. 'What a pity you're only going to be with us for a short time— life here might have become far more interesting!'

His eyes were running over her admiringly as he spoke, but Leigh was taking little notice, she was too busy wondering just what Bruce Allerton was playing at.

'When are you starting?' Don Chapman asked her.

'Tomorrow morning. Brighton first and then Scotland.'

A quickly hidden flash of amusement showed in the older man's face, which puzzled Leigh, especially when she saw that Mike Stewart was grinning, too.

She was tempted to ask why, but the chance was lost when Vic Parker, the chief mechanic, said to Allerton, 'That rep from the spares firm should be here at any minute. You said you wanted to discuss the list first.'

'Yes, I know. Unfortunately this interview took me longer than I intended.' He turned to Leigh. 'If you go and see Carol, the receptionist, she'll tell you how to get to the Beechwood. See you tomorrow,' he added, nodding dismissively.

But Leigh wasn't going to be put off quite that easily. 'I'd like to speak to you alone for a moment first.'

He frowned. 'You've just heard that I'm busy.'

She stood her ground. 'Nevertheless, I should like to speak to you.'

'Oh, very well. Shan't be more than a minute, Vic.'

Leigh walked out into the corridor ahead of him and turned to face him as soon as he had closed the door.

'I'm quite sure you know what I want to say,' she informed him, making no pretence of hiding her anger.

'But how can I possibly imagine how a mind like yours works, Miss Bishop?' he answered mockingly.

Somehow Leigh stifled the impulse to be really

rude and demanded, 'Just why did you tell those men that I'd only be working for you for a short time?'

Bryce Allerton smiled sardonically. 'You know, you really should read the small print before you sign anything, Miss Bishop. When I saw the sneaky trick you pulled to get this job and the threats you were making to keep it, I decided that I could be as tricky as you were. So when I left you for a few minutes before the flight, I told Carol to type in a couple of extra clauses to your contract.'

Her cheeks gone suddenly pale, Leigh said stiltedly, 'What clauses?'

Lifting up his fingers he ticked them off. 'The first, that you're here on only one month's trial, instead of three. The second,' his smile changed into a sneer, 'that if you cause any disruption among my staff or upset any of them in any way, then you're out—immediately.' He leaned towards her. 'And as I count myself as a member of the staff, I don't somehow think you're going to last very long, do you?'

CHAPTER TWO

LEIGH had been born with the sort of temper that went with chestnut hair and green eyes, but over the years she had largely learnt to control it. Now, however, it took an almost superhuman effort of will not to tell this arrogant pig of a man just what he could do with his precious job. Colour flooded into her cheeks and she would have given a great deal to be able to hit him in his stupid, grinning face. Instead, she just turned away and left him standing there, laughing at her, and pushed through the door into the reception area. The girl, Carol, was talking on the phone, but after a few moments she replaced the receiver and turned to Leigh, her face as full of sharp curiosity as the men's had been.

'I've booked a room for you at the Beechwood. I wasn't sure whether you wanted a single or a double, but they have both available, so you can tell them when you get there. Is that all right?'

'Yes, thank you,' Leigh answered mechanically, her mind still fulminating about the way Bryce Allerton had tricked her.

'Which did you want, a single or a double?'

'What?' Leigh looked at the girl and realised she was trying to pump her. 'Oh, I'll make up my mind when I see the rooms.'

'Here's the hotel's address. Do you know the area?'

'No, I've never been here before.'

'I'd better draw you a map, then.'

Carol picked up a piece of paper and sketched the route she had to take, pointing out landmarks to look for.

'Thank you very much; I'm sure I'll be able to find it. Goodbye.'

The girl looked rather affronted when Leigh picked up the sketch and left, and it wasn't until she was driving along in the car trying to find the hotel that Leigh realised that she had been rather abrupt with the receptionist. She supposed that as a new member of the staff she ought to have introduced herself properly and made some effort to be pleasant and get to know the other girl, but she had been so steamed up over Bryce Allerton that she hadn't even given it a thought. Leigh sighed. Well, it was too late now, she'd just have to try and smooth over any bad impression she'd made the next time they met. Especially as she thought that she was going to need a friend at Allerton's, even though it now seemed as if she was going to be there for a much shorter time than she had anticipated.

The Beechwood was a large Victorian house that had been converted into a hotel with the help of several modern additions that seemed to extend from all sides of it, but as it stood back from the road and had some garden and trees left on both sides, the finished appearance was still quite pleasant. After enquiring the prices of the rooms, Leigh didn't bother to ask to see the double, she had to settle for the single because it was considerably cheaper. She found out why when she was shown up to it. The room was on the second floor at the back, a box of a room only about ten feet square with a window overlooking a courtyard that seemed to house nothing but dustbins. But the bed looked comfortable; there was a hand basin in the corner, and some effort had been made to brighten the place up with pretty wallpaper and matching curtains. Leigh explained about the early morning starts she would have to make, but the manager said they had had pilots staying before and promised to give her an early morning call and to make sure that the front door was unlocked so that she could get out. He made no promises about breakfast, though, and Leigh could hardly blame him; it wasn't worth paying a chef to come in so early for just one guest. So it looked as if she would have to go out and do some shopping if she wanted breakfast the next morning.

She began to unpack the suitcases she had brought with her from her home in Devon, but halfway through the job reaction set in and she sat down on the bed, feeling desolate and lonely. But Leigh had been alone in hotel rooms many times before and she soon fought down the feeling, realising that it resulted directly from the churlish way that she had been treated by Bryce Allerton. It was obvious that he hadn't believed that the mix-up over her name had been a genuine misunderstanding and she could understand him being angry, but surely not to the extent that he had been. Maybe it was because he was one of the large group of men who believed that there was no place for women in flying except as stewardesses; glorified waitresses who worked damned hard dispensing food and

drink, and charming the passengers into forgetting
their fears that these great lumps of metal just
wouldn't stay in the sky long enough to get them
where they were going. It was an attitude Leigh
had met many times before, especially among
younger pilots, strangely enough; the older ones
were more inclined to be indulgent, probably because they were well established in their jobs and
didn't see women as any threat to their careers.

Leigh sighed, got up and resumed unpacking,
putting her clothes neatly away in drawers and
wardrobe. It seemed, then, that this job was not
going to last her more than a month at the most,
which would not only see her on the dole queue
again but would leave a question mark on her
record. How many prospective employers, she
wondered, would believe that she was sacked
simply because her boss didn't like women pilots?
But she needed money badly. After several months
on the dole all her savings had been used up and
she still owed her share of three months' upkeep
and payment on a Tiger Moth that she shared with
three other enthusiasts, and she had also had to
borrow money from her father because Allerton's
paid their employees monthly and she would have
to keep herself for the four weeks until she got
paid. If she lasted out the four weeks, that was.
Having crossed swords with Mr Bryce Allerton,
she wouldn't be surprised if he didn't cook up some
excuse and have her out within a couple of days!

When she had finished unpacking, Leigh drove
into Shepton Ferrers to buy some groceries. It was
a typical new town, well laid out with wide roads
and grass verges, the industrial and residential

areas set apart, and with a large central shopping
mall of the new precinct type hidden behind acres
of glass and concrete; comfortable to shop in
during the winter or when it rained, but hateful in
the summer. Because it was so new the trees lining
the verges and the gardens outside the rows of
terrace houses hadn't yet had time to grow and
mellow the stark look of the new brick and concrete. In time, when the parks and playing fields
were established, it would be a very pleasant place
to live in, but right now it looked what it was, a
planning design that was gradually coming to life,
its priorities given to houses, work and shops, with
recreational and leisure pursuits coming only a
slow second.

Rather than run the risk of being tempted by the
clothes shops in the precinct, Leigh bought the
things she needed at a small corner shop in a village
a mile or so from the hotel, a village of small, old,
terraced cottages that used the few fields around it
as a barrier against the encroachment of the new
town. Only a couple of miles away in distance but
a whole world away in atmosphere and surroundings. That evening she ate in the hotel, the
food substantial enough but not very inspiring, and
went to bed very early so that she'd be up in time
to get to the airport by five o'clock.

Leigh wasn't very good at getting up early, but
once she was up she was fully awake, and at least
at that hour she didn't have to fight for the bathroom. She breakfasted off muesli and long-life
milk, and made herself a couple of ham rolls to eat
later on. A cup of coffee would have been heaven,
and she wished now that she had brought the elec-

tric kettle from her old digs with her, but there hadn't really been room in the car, and anyway, she'd thought that she'd have plenty of time to collect the rest of her things at a later date. Leigh laughed mirthlessly to herself; now it seemed as if she would be going back home any day now, thanks to Bryce Allerton. Oh, well, at least it would save her a journey.

The thought of Bryce Allerton needled her all the way to the airport and she had to consciously make herself put him out of her mind. It wasn't good to start a day of flying when you were tense and had problems on your mind; that way only led to carelessness and accidents. But, fortunately, he wasn't around when she arrived; after she had filed her flight plan there was only Vic Parker out on the tarmac, standing by the plane. It was a twin-engined job which had once been used for passengers but had now had all the seats taken out so that it could be used for freight.

'Have you had much experience of carrying freight?' Vic asked her.

Leigh shook her head. 'Not a great deal. And when I did it was mostly small stuff.'

'Well, just remember that the cargo must be distributed very carefully because of the centre of gravity, and make sure that everything is safely tied down. Don't let the loaders go until you're satisfied,' he warned.

He told her who to contact when she picked up the cargo of vegetables at Brighton and added another word or two of advice for which Leigh thanked him sincerely, glad that at least everyone wasn't against her.

It began to rain as Leigh climbed into the
cockpit, the April skies grey with heavy cloud. Not
ideal flying weather by any means, but at least
in a plane you could get above the clouds and up
into the sun. She dropped her heavy flight bag,
full of charts, documents, calculator etc., on the
empty seat beside her and went carefully through
all the pre-flight checks, mentally going over
everything twice to make absolutely sure, then
she called up the control tower and took off
shortly after, the cloud base now down to twelve
hundred feet. The plane climbed steadily through
the dirty cotton wool of the cloud; easy and
light to handle now that it was empty, emerging at
last, with startling comparison, into the bright clear
blue sky above, the morning sun shining into her
left-hand window as she headed south for
Brighton.

Leigh arrived in Brighton in plenty of time and
didn't have too much difficulty in locating her
cargo, thanks to Vic Parker's instructions. It was
still very early in the morning, but even so there
was still a great deal of activity at the airport:
lorries constantly arriving to deliver or collect
goods from the various warehouses, passengers
hurrying out eagerly to waiting planes, or more
slowly disembarking, looking tired and untidy after
extremely early starts, private planes or air taxis
bringing people in for Brighton races. It was a-
capsule of life, busy, but highly organised and efficient. Leigh went to get herself a much-needed
coffee in the snack bar and sat by the window
overlooking the tarmac, taking everything in
greedily, not realising until now quite how much

she had missed all this during her months out of work.

The trailer with her cargo drove across to the plane and Leigh quickly drained her coffee so that she could hurry over and supervise the loading. The vegetables were onions! Leigh could smell them when she was still some distance away. And there were sacks and sacks of them. The trailer driver and his mate pulled up beside the plane and looked round expectantly for the pilot. Leigh walked up to them and said in dismay, 'Are they all onions?'

'No,' the senior man replied. 'There are a few crates of French cabbage and one of garlic.' He looked her over. 'Are you something to do with Allerton's?'

Leigh nodded, still appalled by the thought of having to fly this load of rank-smelling vegetables all the way to Scotland.

'Do you know where the pilot is, then?'

Ruefully she admitted, 'I am the pilot.'

The two men looked at her in astonishment and exclaimed in surprise, but Leigh took little notice; she was used to that reaction and had become immune to it over the years. She was remembering now the looks of amusement on the faces of the other two Allerton pilots yesterday when she'd told them which run she was doing. No wonder they'd thought it funny!

'How long have you been flying?' the driver was demanding.

'Long enough,' Leigh answered shortly. 'Come on, let's get it aboard.'

She climbed into the plane through the cargo door and watched closely as the men loaded the

vegetables, but her supervision was largely un-
necessary, both the men were experienced at handling air freight and knew exactly how to dispose
the crates and sacks to keep the plane properly
balanced. By the time they had finished Leigh was
glad to get out and stand in the fresh air again for
a few minutes; the smell in the confined space of
the plane was overwhelming and already her eyes
were starting to water.

This fact worried her as she took her seat in the
cockpit, it could be dangerous trying to fly the
plane when her eyes were continuously streaming,
but the door between the cockpit and the cabin
fitted tightly and the smell wasn't quite so bad in
here. Even so, Leigh could well imagine it getting
worse as time went on and she wondered what
other pilots had done on the same trip. That it was
a regular pick-up seemed likely from the way Mike
Stewart and Don Chapman had reacted. The only
thing Leigh could think of was some sort of mask
to fit over her nose. Her immediate thought was of
an oxygen mask, but this plane didn't fly high
enough to need them, and wasn't fitted with them.
But it gave her an idea and she got up to open the
first aid box and delve inside. Sure enough, among
the usual stock of medicaments, slings, splints and
other items considered vital to carry on a plane,
was a box of formed gauze masks that fitted over
the nose and mouth and tied at the back of the
head, provided, presumably, in case of smoke or
chemical fumes leaking into the cockpit. Leigh
noted with some satisfaction that the box was half
empty, proving that others had found it necessary
to use them before—not that either of the other

pilots had pointed this out to her, of course. For a moment she was angry, then shrugged resignedly; as a newcomer she could expect to get the worst jobs and to have jokes played on her. Ordinarily it wouldn't have mattered too much and she would have taken it all in her stride, but with Bryce Allerton breathing down her neck and looking for any excuse to get rid of her, it just made life that much more difficult.

She took off from Brighton without any trouble, although she had to learn to handle the plane all over again now that it was fully loaded. There were a few other planes in sight near the coast, but as Leigh flew north the sky emptied until she came to the difficult area around Gatwick, London's second largest airport, where she had to concentrate closely on the instructions given over the radio as she flew through the controlled airspace. Then there were only the smaller airfields to contend with as she passed from one radio beacon to another, gradually travelling north. After a couple of hours the pungent odour of the onions seeped into the cockpit and she had to put on the mask to stop her eyes watering. A great way to travel; and she thought of that odious man Bryce Allerton with increasing venom. At Carlisle she came down to refuel and took off again almost at once, heading for Dalcross Airport, just outside Inverness.

As she drew nearer she asked for a weather report and wasn't surprised to hear, 'Cloud base between six and seven hundred feet above sea level over the entire area. Visibility two kilometres in rain and lessening.'

'Weather copied,' Leigh answered automatically.

'Could I have the regional pressure setting, please?'

'Nine nine eight millibars.'

'Nine nine eight,' she repeated, setting the figure on the altimeter scale.

Circling to come into the wind, she flew down from the sun brushing through the misty grey clouds and coming in over the restless, rainswept greyness of the Moray Firth, to land sedately on the puddled tarmac and taxi round towards the airport buildings. Leaving the agent to unload the cargo, and the cockpit door wide open to get rid of the stink, Leigh sprinted across to the airport buildings to get some coffee to drink with her rolls. As she stood in line she noticed the people near her giving her funny looks and one or two of them flinched away. With a feeling of foreboding, Leigh unobtrusively sniffed at her jacket and realised that the onion and garlic smells had permeated her clothes! In her last job she had always worn a uniform, very similar to a stewardess's, and she had automatically turned up for work today in clothes as near that as she could: a neat navy suit with pleated skirt and fitted jacket which was brand new, bought on the strength of getting this job. It had just never occurred to her to wear old clothes because she might get dirty or smelly. But now the suit would have to be cleaned before she could possibly wear it again, an expense she could ill afford until she got paid.

Collecting her coffee, she hurried to sit by herself in a corner, feeling as if she'd got B.O. When she thought that the men had had sufficient time to unload, she went out in the rain again to supervise the loading of the new cargo. It was fish—strong, dankly salt-smelling fish! Leigh looked at the crates being stored aboard and for a few seconds indulged in the very pleasant pastime of thinking just what she'd like to do to Bryce Allerton, which included telling him exactly and in detail what he could do with his rotten onions and fish. A large drop of rain landed on her forehead, trickled down and off the end of her nose. And suddenly she saw the funny side of it and, leaning against the plane she began to laugh rather hysterically, much to the wonder of the men who were loading the plane, who looked at her as if she was mad.

Well, at least the reek of fish wouldn't make her cry, Leigh thought as she took off her sopping wet headscarf and settled down into the pilot's seat, and with any luck it might even kill the smell of the onions. So, feeling in a more relaxed and cheerful frame of mind simply because she couldn't envisage things getting worse, she began the long haul south again to Stansted. Her pick-ups and deliveries so far had gone without a hitch, and she had to admit that, if nothing else, Allerton Air Charters were efficient. Their planes, too, were well looked after; this one handled beautifully even though it was quite an old plane, and all the instruments were working perfectly.

It was almost five in the evening before Leigh flew into Shepton Ferrers, tired and hungry. But there was still the plane's log and her pilot's log to write up, and the receipts she had collected for the cargo to hand in before she could go home and change out of her smelly clothes. Handing over the plane to Vic Parker, she went across to the glass doors leading into the crew room and walked in. The room wasn't very large, only about twenty feet square but it was pleasantly decorated and furnished with a small desk, four big armchairs, a table with more chairs round it, a coffee machine, and a radio and television set built into a unit in the corner. At the moment that was all the room contained, there weren't any other crew members about, so Leigh gave a sigh of relief and sat down at the desk to write her reports. Her eyes were drawn to the walls which were covered in the usual mass of Civil Aviation Authority regulations, a map of the surrounding area, framed weather charts, and various notices. Those were all the official things; the unofficial ones included a great many magazine and newspaper cartoons about flying in one aspect or another, some long and derisory poems on the same subject and several calendar-type pin-ups, including a large poster showing the outline of the back view of a very shapely girl wearing nothing but very high-heeled shoes and a pair of panties—which she was just starting to pull down. The caption, in very large letters, said, 'Get 'em down safely with Air Traffic Control'.

Leigh looked at it grimly, then turned quickly as the door opened and the two pilots, Mike Stewart and Don Chapman, entered. They both gave her quick, speculative glances as they came in, but Leigh took the wind out of their sails by giving them a bright smile and saying, 'Hallo there.'

'Hallo.' Mike Stewart smiled back and strolled over to her, to sit on the edge of the desk she was using. 'How did it go?'

'Oh, fine,' Leigh answered heartily. 'Pick-ups and deliveries went off without a hitch.'

'Good.' He leant close enough to get a whiff of her clothes and failed to hide the laughter in his eyes. 'What was the weather like in Scotland?'

'Rain and low cloud base; pretty much what you'd expect for this time of year. How about you?' she added. 'What have you two been doing today?'

'Well, I flew a couple of film people over to Monte Carlo for a conference and sunbathed on the beach while I waited for them. And Don,' he turned to look at Don Chapman who was placidly filling his pipe, 'you took some stuff over to Belgium, didn't you?'

'How pleasant,' Leigh remarked calmly, knowing that Mike was deliberately turning the knife in the wound. So she added with gentle irony, 'I used to do those runs all the time with South-East Air.'

'Ah, yes, the joys of scheduled flights.'

'Have you ever done any?' she asked innocently. Mike's smile tightened and she heard Don Chapman give a laugh which he turned into a cough. But Mike ducked the issue by saying with mocking gallantry, 'Never with anyone as beautiful as you in the co-pilot's seat.'

He leaned over her as he said it and, of course, Bryce Allerton chose just that moment to walk into the room. He glowered at them and Leigh found herself flushing at the sight of him, all the dislike she felt rushing back. Mike quickly moved away and Bryce came over to her.

'Good evening,' he said coldly. 'You're supposed to report into the reception desk as soon as you arrive.'

'If you'd told me I had to previously I would have done so,' Leigh retorted in a voice that was equally glacial.

'Let's have your receipts.'

She handed them to him and he flicked through them.

'Have you made your logs and report out yet?'

'I'm working on them now.'

'Give them to Carol as soon as you've finished. Did you have any trouble with the plane?'

'No, it handled beautifully.'

'And you found the agents all right?'

'Yes.'

'And the cargoes?'

Leigh chose not to understand. 'What about the cargoes?'

'They didn't give you any trouble?'

'What trouble could they give me? They were all properly loaded and secured, if that's what you mean.'

'It wasn't.' He looked down at her sardonically and then wrinkled his nose in very obvious distaste. 'They would appear to have had an extremely strong smell.'

'Really?' Leigh raised green eyes that were wide and innocent to look into his mocking grey ones. 'I'm afraid I wouldn't know. You see, I have no sense of smell!'

For a fraction of a second his eyes widened in stunned surprise and Leigh mentally chalked up the victory in that round, but then his face changed and he said bitingly, 'In that case you won't mind doing that run every time, will you?'

There was no chance of hiding the chagrin in her face from him and he gave her a look of cool, satisfied amusement before he turned away.

Addressing the three of them in general, he said, 'Here's the roster for the rest of the week.'

The others went over to look and he talked to them about it for some minutes. Leigh, her head down as she tried to concentrate on her notes, noticed that the pilots called him Bryce and seemed to be on easy, friendly terms with him. But then they were men, weren't they? she thought resentfully. After five minutes or so he left and Mike came over to her again.

'How about coming out for a drink when you're through?'

Leigh laughed rather ruefully. 'Thanks, but I'm not very nice to be with at the moment, as you very well know.'

He grinned. 'Haven't you really got any sense of smell?'

'Of course I have. I just didn't want Mr Allerton to think he'd got away with it, that's all.' She sighed. 'But now it looks as if I'm landed with the run. Hoist with my own petard, or whatever the cliché is.'

'I shouldn't worry, Leigh,' Don Chapman joined in. 'All the new pilots get that run for the first few weeks, then we take it in turns.'

'Only it doesn't look as if I'll be here that long, does it?' Leigh remarked, unable to keep the bitterness out of her voice.

The two pilots looked at one another and Don Chapman said mildly, 'He has his reasons.'

'Just because I turned out to be a woman instead of a man.'

'That's one of the reasons, certainly, but not the biggest, and certainly not the most important.' Leigh looked at him expectantly, but he merely straightened up and said, 'Well, I'm off. I've an early start in the morning. Coming, Mike?' he added pointedly.

Mike Stewart hesitated for a moment, looking at Leigh, but she bent her head over her reports again and he shrugged. 'Might as well.'

They left her alone and she was able to finish her task, writing neatly and clearly. Then she made a note of her job tomorrow: taking a cargo of machine tools to Manchester, then over to Liverpool for another load to take to Cambridge. The other two men, she noted, were both doing air-taxi work, taking passengers abroad. There were also the names of two other pilots on the roster that she hadn't yet met, making five pilots in all, although Don, of course, was part-time.

There was no one at the reception desk when she left, so she put the log books in the 'IN' tray and drove wearily back to the hotel, where she gratefully showered and washed the smell out of her hair, putting her clothes into a polythene bag and leaving them in the car so that they wouldn't stink her room out. As soon as she could she'd have to take them to an express cleaners. She bought a Chinese takeaway and ate it in her room, because it was cheaper than the hotel dining-room, then got ready for bed and lay awake for a while, unable to get Bryce Allerton out of her mind as she wondered what other reason he could possibly have for disliking her so much.

The next morning Leigh didn't have to report in until seven. She arrived wearing a sweater, casual jacket and cord jeans this time, her hair and body clean and sweet-smelling again. If she wasn't going to fly any passengers then there was no point in taking the risk of having her good clothes ruined. She was given the same plane to fly and, on the tarmac, met the other two pilots, one of whom had worked for Laker Airways and been made redundant when it folded and so was a comparative newcomer to Allerton's, and the other who had flown for the company almost since it was formed and was close to retirement age. Both of them were married, and both of them treated her as if she was some sort of freak, definitely not to be taken seriously.

Her work that day was uneventful, the pick-ups were well organised and she again ate a snack lunch while she was waiting for a cargo to be unloaded, but today she had brought a small flask with her which she had filled from the coffee machine in the crew room. Arriving back at Shepton Ferrers, Leigh took her receipts out to the reception desk and gave them to Carol. 'Hallo,' she said with a smile, 'I understand I have to give these direct to you?'

She was greeted with a cold look and, 'Mr Allerton wants to see you in his office right away.'

The other girl had made no attempt to take the papers Leigh was holding out to her and had spoken so insolently that Leigh was taken aback, as one always is when one meets unexpected rudeness. After a moment, she silently put the receipts

down on the desk and went slowly up the stairs to
Bryce Allerton's office, wondering what was
coming, wondering if he was going to sack her
already. Outside his door she hesitated, gathering
herself to face him, and he opened the door just as
she lifted her hand to knock. For a moment they
stared at each other silently, then both started to
speak at once.

'Carol said you wanted to see me . . .'

'Come in, I want to talk to you . . .'

Their voices trailed off and Leigh felt her heart
begin to beat loudly in her chest. Bryce moved
aside and motioned for her to enter.

Leigh walked into the room and turned to wait
for him. He closed the door and walked over to
the desk, his hands thrust in his pockets. Neither
of them made any attempt to sit down. Bryce
looked her over for a long moment, the coldness in
his eyes making Leigh cringe inside.

Abruptly he said, 'Are you deliberately trying to
provoke me, or are you just naturally careless and
forgetful?'

Leigh stared at him in astonishment. 'I don't
know what you mean.'

'Really?' There was a world of disbelief in his
tone. 'Last night I asked you to hand in your logs
to Carol when you'd finished them.'

'That's right. I did.'

His left eyebrow rose. 'You gave them to her
personally?'

'No, there was no one at the desk. I supposed
she must have gone home, so I put them in the
'IN' tray.'

'Then just how,' he demanded harshly, 'do you

account for the fact that Carol couldn't find them when she came in this morning, and they were eventually located by one of the cleaners who almost threw them away thinking they were rubbish?'

'Where did she find them?' Leigh asked, her face pale.

'On the floor underneath one of the armchairs in the crew room. And if that wasn't bad enough, you dare to turn in logs in this disgraceful state!'

Angrily he opened the logs at the page where she had made her entries, and to her consternation Leigh saw that the clean pages were now ringed with coffee beaker stains and there was a large blob of ink over part of her neat entry. She stared at the marks, realising that someone really had it in for her. And the person who most wanted to get rid of her was of course Bryce Allerton himself. But that he should go to such underhand lengths was contemptible.

Raising her head she said distinctly, 'I put the logs in the tray in reception when I left last night and the books were then pristine clean, as you damn well know!'

His head jerked up as he glared at her. 'Don't you swear at me, my girl!'

'I am *not* your girl. And I shall swear as much as I damn well like,' Leigh retorted defiantly. 'I know you want to get rid of me—but to resort to such a mean, sneaky trick as this is despicable!' She glared at him, bright spots of anger in her cheeks, her eyes flashing like the green fire of emeralds. 'All right,' she went on furiously, 'so you've got the excuse to get rid of me that you wanted, even if you did manufacture it yourself. And no matter how much I needed this job, I'm glad to go. I don't know how *anyone* can work for someone who stoops as low as you do!'

She headed for the door, brushing past him contemptuously, but Bryce put out a hand to grab her arm, swinging her round to face him.

'Are you saying you didn't deface those logs?'

'You know darn well I didn't,' Leigh returned hotly.

'No, I *don't* know!' he shouted, his fingers tightening on her arm in fury.

His raised voice brought her up short and Leigh stood there silently, trembling with anger, her heart beating wildly, so mad that she couldn't even speak. Bryce was glaring down at her. He was very close, his hand gripping her like a steel band. For a few moments he continued to glare at her angrily, but then his face changed and he abruptly let her go and turned away.

'That's quite a temper you've got,' he remarked dryly. When Leigh didn't answer he faced her and said acidly, 'I didn't fix those logs to make an excuse to get rid of you. Whether you did it or not I don't know, but they were your responsibility. And I'm warning you that I won't tolerate carelessness or slackness in paperwork because it usually means carelessness and slackness in flying too. So watch it in future.'

Leigh looked at him rather dazedly. 'You mean you're not firing me?'

'Not this time, no.' He held out the logs to her. 'Now take these and clean them up.'

Slowly she walked towards him and took the

books from him. Raising her head, she looked him in the eyes and said, 'If you didn't someone else must have done. With two people at Allerton's against me I really don't stand much of a chance, do I?'

CHAPTER THREE

WHEN Leigh came out of Bryce Allerton's office, she carefully shut the door behind her and then had to lean against the wall for a few minutes to try and control the tremors of rage that still shook her. She could never remember having been so angry in her life. But she had really believed that he was going to sack her and so had given full rein to her highly volatile temper. It wasn't a thing that happened often, she'd learnt to keep it well under control, but the thought that he could pull such a dirty trick had made her just blow up. But the strange thing was that once he had assured her that he hadn't done it, she had believed him, without hesitation or any further doubts. Which meant, as she had said, that there was someone else who wanted her out. And that could only be one other person.

Slowly Leigh straightened up and made her way back down to the reception area. Carol looked up as soon as she came in, her eyes bright with avid curiosity, then quickly away again. Leigh walked over to the desk and waited patiently while the other girl fidgeted around with some papers, deliberately making her wait. Then she at last looked up and said impatiently, 'Yes?'

Smothering a flicker of anger, Leigh answered persuasively, 'I'm afraid we seem to have started off rather badly, and if it's my fault then I'm sorry.'

She smiled placatingly and went on, 'I really would like to be friends—especially as we seem to be the only two women among all these males.'

Carol looked at her for a moment while Leigh waited hopefully, then dashed most of her hopes by saying, 'I don't know what you mean.'

Leigh ought to have left it then, but she persevered because she hated to work in an uncomfortable atmosphere. 'I just thought that we could get to know one another a bit more, and, as I'm a stranger here, perhaps you could tell me the places to go. We might even go to a disco or something together one night.'

A spiteful look came into Carol's eyes as she said nastily, 'Unlike you, my taste doesn't run to girls—I like going out with men!'

For a second Leigh didn't get it, but then her eyes widened in shock. 'Why you disgusting-minded little . . .' She abruptly bit off what she was going to say, aware that she was lowering herself to the other girl's level. Swinging on her heel, she walked quickly back to the crew room, almost knocking Mike Stewart down as she strode in.

'Hey, what's the rush?' he demanded, putting out a hand to steady her as she stumbled against him.

'Oh, sorry, Mike.' She went to sit at the desk, trying to pull herself together but still seething with anger.

'What's up?' Mike asked again. 'You look as if you'd like to hit somebody.'

'Yes, I would,' Leigh agreed. 'I'd like that very much.'

He pretended to look dismayed. 'I'd better get out of range, then!'

'What?' Leigh realised that he was teasing her and some of her anger evaporated as she smiled at him. 'That's right, you ought to shake in your shoes. I pack quite a punch when I get riled!'

'Glad I'm not on the receiving end, then. Who made you angry?'

'Oh, no one in particular.'

'You can tell your Uncle Mike, you know,' he told her with an engaging grin. 'Always got a shoulder available for distressed young ladies to cry on.'

'Thanks,' Leigh returned lightly, 'but it was nothing, really.'

His eyebrows rose sceptically. 'You don't look as if it was nothing, which means that you don't trust me.'

Leigh shook her head. 'I prefer to fight my own battles, that's all.'

He straightened from where he'd been perched on the edge of the desk. 'Well, if you ever find you need reinforcements, you know where to find me.' He nodded in farewell. 'So long, see you tomorrow.'

'Goodnight, Mike.'

When he'd gone, Leigh wondered why she hadn't confided in him; Mike had certainly seemed friendly and approachable. But perhaps it was because he had been just a little too eager that she had drawn back from confiding in him. That, and a natural reluctance to repeat the remark that Carol had made. With an unhappy sigh, she opened the log books to clean them up as best she could and write up the day's report. And when she had done she made sure that one of the other pilots was with her so that she had a witness when she handed the books over to Carol.

Fortunately the next three days passed without incident. She flew more freight around the country and didn't get any passengers to carry or any very interesting places to go to, but she didn't mind that at all, at least she was still in a job. The other pilots were pleasant enough to her, Mike especially so, although everyone seemed to be so busy that she didn't see any of them for any length of time. So whether or not Carol had started to spread any rumours, Leigh just couldn't tell. As for Bryce Allerton, Leigh kept a wary eye open for him and kept out of his way as much as possible.

Late on Friday afternoon, however, he sought her out just after she'd flown in from a trip to Cardiff. Leigh was out on the tarmac talking to Vic Parker about the plane and there was quite a lot of noise coming from the nearby hangar, so she didn't hear Bryce approaching. He touched her on her arm to gain her attention and she nearly jumped out of her skin when she saw who it was.

He looked at her in some surprise, then said sardonically, 'Guilty conscience?'

Shaking her head, Leigh replied shortly, 'I just don't like people creeping up behind me, that's all.'

His eyes narrowed, but he let it go, nodding at Vic and saying, 'If you've finished, I'd like a word with Miss Bishop.'

'Sure,' Vic answered. 'We were just talking about the tyres, but they're good for a few landings yet. She's light on the planes,' he added, looking directly at Bryce.

That compliment helped Leigh, even though her boss seemed to take no notice of it. He led her a few steps to one side and said abruptly, 'I know you're supposed to have this weekend off, but I've had someone phone in to hire a plane and pilot for Sunday. He wants the plane for most of the day.'

'He?'

'Yes, some kind of amateur archaeologist, from what I can gather. The job's yours if you want it. It will be at overtime rates, of course.'

'Th-thank you,' Leigh stammered, not quite sure how to take the offer, but glad of the opportunity to make some extra money.

Bryce's eyebrows rose derisively. 'Don't read something into this that isn't there. Don Chapman usually does this sort of odd job for me, but I'm still one pilot short, so he's been working full time and wants to keep the weekend free. And all the other men have something fixed up, so it was either you or turn the job down.'

'I see,' Leigh answered stiffly.

'So don't go thinking that anything's changed,' Bryce advised her. 'You're still on your way out as far as I'm concerned.'

'Oh, you've made that very clear. I'm hardly likely to forget.'

She was about to turn away when he remarked, 'You got back from Cardiff quickly.'

Shrugging, Leigh answered, 'It was a quick turn-around. There was nothing to hang around for.'

'How long were you on the ground at Cardiff?'

'Not more than an hour at the most.'

'And you supervised the loading yourself?'

'Yes.' Leigh looked at him with some misgiving,

wondering what he was leading up to. 'But there were only four crates and I made quite sure they were stowed safely,' she said defensively.

A slight frown came into his eyes as he looked at her taut face, then he surprised her by saying, 'I didn't suggest they weren't. I just want to know how, when you were only on the ground for an hour, you found the time to have a meal?'

Leigh's eyes flew wide in surprise, and without thinking she exclaimed, 'Why on earth should *you* care whether or not I have a meal?'

He frowned again and snapped out, 'You know as well as I do that going without food for long periods slows down your reactions, it can even make you giddy. I've noticed that not one day this week have you given yourself time to eat a proper meal. You can't be dieting, because you're skinny enough already,' he added, his eyes running over her. 'So that must mean you're trying to impress me by clipping time off the runs. Well, it doesn't,' he told her baldly. 'I don't appreciate pilots fainting from hunger when they're flying my planes.'

'Oh, for heaven's sake!' Leigh exclaimed as soon as she could get a word in. 'I am not starving myself, and I'm *certainly* not trying to impress you. I'm quite sure that would be impossible! I just don't like having a big meal at lunch times; I prefer to eat in the evening. But I always have something.'

'What?'

'I take coffee and rolls with me and eat them either in the airport lounge or in the plane.'

He continued to look at her rather sceptically, but then nodded curtly. 'See you do have something. And take your time over it. You're entitled to an hour's break at lunch time.'

With that he turned and walked back to the Allerton building, leaving Leigh with strangely mixed feelings; surprised that he'd even noticed that she wasn't taking a lunch break, and vaguely resentful because he'd called her skinny. But at least it proved that he was checking her logs and watching her closely, still ready to pounce whenever she made a mistake.

All day Saturday Leigh spent looking for some cheaper digs because the hotel charged really more than she could afford, but all she did was waste a lot of time following up adverts in the local newspaper by telephone or car. There were very few places available, and those that were turned her down as soon as they found out that she might sometimes have to go to work very early in the morning. Discouraged, Leigh returned to the hotel and spent Saturday night writing to her parents and various friends.

The amateur archaeologist was already waiting for her when Leigh arrived at the airport the next morning. He was one of those mild-mannered sort of men who always got their own way because you felt sorry for them. After his first look of dismay when he found he had a woman pilot, he showed her some maps he had brought with him and indicated several sites over a wide area where he thought ancient, lost villages or settlements had once stood, and which he wanted to fly over and photograph.

'There are rather a lot of sites,' Leigh remarked dubiously. 'Are you sure you want to do them all in one day?'

'Oh, yes. The light's just right. I'm sure if we went up straight away we'd have plenty of time.'

'Well, we'll try. Let me sort out my maps and charts.'

'Won't these do?' he asked impatiently.

'I'm afraid not. Pilots have special charts showing all the radio beacons and airways. And I expect you'll want me to fly pretty low, so we have to make sure we're not intruding in any R.A.F. low-level zone.'

He tried to hurry her, but Leigh took her time over planning the order of the sites he wanted to look at, working out the best way to do it to save time and fuel. One of Vic Parker's mechanics had the Arrow all ready for them and the archaeologist climbed eagerly in beside her, wanting to be off and fussing and fidgeting while she went through the pre-flight checks.

It took much longer than she had expected because the man insisted on flying over each site at least four times until they were at the right height and the right angle for his camera. But he was polite about it and Leigh swallowed any feeling of irritation and did her best for him; after all, he was the customer and was paying for the flight. Towards midday they began to get rather low on fuel and Leigh suggested they return to the airport.

'But this next site is only a few miles away,' the man protested. 'It would take hardly any petrol at all to go there.'

'But we'll be heading into the wind,' Leigh pointed out.

The archaeologist, however, had no idea whatsoever of the difficulties of flying. To him the air outside was just emptiness, he couldn't begin to imagine that it had currents that were stronger than a sea tide, that it was tough and resistant. Because he couldn't see the air he thought it didn't exist. He pleaded to go on so urgently that, against her better judgment, Leigh did as he asked. And, of course, once he saw the site he got so enthusiastic that nothing would satisfy him but to fly over it half a dozen times. Leigh kept her turns as tight as she could, then purposefully headed for home in a dead straight line. The petrol was getting far too low, not dangerously so, of course, but you always needed some in reserve to leave room for manoeuvre. In the air you never knew when an emergency might crop up. She just made it to the airport without having to use her fuel boost pump, and taxied over to the hangar with a sigh of relief.

Her passenger climbed out first and said excitedly, 'I'll change the film in the camera and we'll go up again as soon as we've refuelled.'

'How about giving the pilot a break first?'

Leigh recognised that curt tone and looked down in surprise as she started to climb out of the cockpit. Instead of Vic's assistant, the white-overalled mechanic preparing to pump petrol into the plane's tanks was Bryce Allerton himself.

'Oh, but it's the light, you know,' the archaeologist was saying. 'Now is the best time of day for aerial photography.'

'Half an hour or so won't make any difference.'

The firmness in Bryce's tone silenced him far more effectively than all Leigh's reasonable arguments had done, and she could only envy such self-assertiveness. Taking her usual flask and rolls from

the cockpit, she walked over to the main building and sat on a bench over against the wall.
The sun, although not yet strong, was pleasant,
and normally Leigh would have enjoyed the break,
but today she only picked at her rolls. Her eyes
were fixed on Bryce Allerton as he refilled the
fuel tanks in the wings of the plane, and she
cursed the fate that had made him come to refuel
it instead of the mechanic, because there was no
way he wasn't going to notice how much petrol he
put in and realise that her tanks had run too
low.

He finished refuelling, stowed all the gear away
safely and then strolled casually across the fifty
yards or so to where she was sitting. Leigh looked
up nervously as he came over, waiting for the ex-
plosion of anger to burst round her head. But he
astounded her by sitting down beside her on the
bench and offering her a pack of cigarettes.

'Smoke?'

Leigh shook her head. 'I don't, thanks.'

'Very wise.' He shook out a cigarette, lit it, then
leaned back against the wall, eyes half closed
against the sun. 'Where did you take him?'

'Mostly around the Northampton area, following the line of the rivers north looking for traces
of old settlements.'

'Did you find any?'

'Yes. There were some he'd already noted on the
ground and wanted to make sure of, and some he
couldn't make up his mind about because the
outlines were too vague.'

'And I suppose he had you flying all round
those to get the shadows right.'

Leigh looked at him in surprise. 'You've taken him up before?'

'No, but I know the type,' he replied brusquely. 'They'd get you flying on your nose if they could.' He turned his head and glanced at her. 'Don't let him bully you.'

'Oh, he doesn't,' Leigh protested. 'He's very polite, and so enthusiastic. You feel you want to help him as much as you can. He said he's trying to get information together for a book and probably wouldn't be able to afford another flight.'

'Nevertheless, don't let him push you too hard. There's more than one way of bullying a person into doing what you want.'

'Well, you should know. After all, you're the expert.'

The moment she had said it, Leigh could have bitten out her tongue. There had been no reason to, in fact quite the opposite, because this was as near as she'd ever got to her extremely unapproachable new boss. But some perverse wish to strike back for his past attitude had made her come out with that barb. He stiffened and stood up, gazing down at her enigmatically. Leigh looked up, an apology forming on her lips, but before she had a chance to speak, he said, 'No matter how much a customer plays on your sympathy, you don't run your tanks that low again. Do you hear me?'

Leigh nodded, aware that she had brought that rebuke on her own head.

Bryce looked down at her coldly, the old disdain back in his eyes. His glance fell on her almost untouched lunch and he said tersely, 'Make sure you eat that before you go up again.'

Leigh tried, but the food stuck in her throat. She was so mad with herself. For once he had almost seemed quite human, and he might not have told her off about the petrol if she hadn't made that stupid remark. Not that it hadn't been justified—he was still the most arrogant man she'd ever met.

The afternoon was much as the morning had been, only they flew more to the east this time, over the flat fields of Cambridgeshire. The air traffic now, though, was much busier. There was a flying school at Shepton Ferrers that had all its planes up, and over on the other side of the airfield were the headquarters of a gliding club and also a microlight or powered hang-glider club. So, as it was a fine day, the air was full and Leigh was glad to get out of the vicinity. The continuous flying up and down eventually became monotonous and tiring, and Leigh was glad when, at six o'clock, the archaeologist decided to call it a day. He thanked her and went off, happily clutching his camera, while Leigh taxied the Arrow over to the hangar.

Bryce arrived just as she climbed out and said, 'Okay, I'll take over.'

'What happened to the mechanic who was here this morning?' Leigh asked idly.

'I had some work to do in the office so didn't see much point in keeping him hanging around all day just to refuel and bed the Arrow down. He was glad enough to take the rest of the day off. I am a qualified mechanic as well as a pilot, if that's what you were wondering,' he added scathingly.

'Not at all,' Leigh returned coldly. 'I just thought

he might have had an accident or something.'

His eyebrows rose quizzically and Leigh had the uncomfortable feeling that he knew darn well that she hadn't thought anything of the sort, that she was just curious to know why he was there, getting his hands dirty and doing a job he obviously didn't have to. Going over to the crew room, she wrote up her logs and report and had almost finished them when Bryce followed her in.

'If you're about finished I'll lock up.'

Obediently Leigh collected her things and preceded him out of the room, dropping the logs into Carol's 'IN' tray ready for tomorrow. At the main door she glanced back and saw that Bryce had picked up the logs and was glancing through them. Checking up on her again, Leigh supposed rather bitterly, and hurried across to her car. Parked beside her Mini was a new three-litre Jaguar. Leigh looked at its sleek, elegant lines enviously, rightly guessing that it belonged to her employer. So Allerton's must be doing really well if he could afford that kind of luxury car. Unless of course it was just a front to impress the customers.

She got into her car and started it up, but had to wait for Bryce to walk past before she could move off. But instead he came over to the Mini and indicated that he wanted to speak to her. Reluctantly Leigh wound down the window. He had to stoop down very low to look at her.

'They don't serve meals on Sundays at your hotel, do they?'

Leigh shook her head, wondering what was coming.

'Have you made any plans for this evening?'

'Why?' she asked cautiously.

A faint flicker of what might have been amusement came into Bryce's grey eyes, but was gone so quickly that she couldn't be sure. 'There's a pub a few miles up the road that does a decent meal. I intend going there myself and wondered if you'd care to come along.'

Now how was she supposed to take that? Leigh wondered. As an invitation to join him for dinner as his guest, or just as a piece of information, take it or leave it?

'Well, I ... er ... um ...' she dithered, completely unsure of whether she wanted to go or not.

'I hope you don't take this long to make a decision when you're flying,' Bryce observed acidly. 'Are you coming or aren't you?'

Goaded, Leigh snapped, 'Yes, I am,' and then realised that she hadn't been going to say that at all. Good grief, she didn't want to spend more time than she absolutely had to in Bryce Allerton's company, did she? But as usual he had made her feel flustered so that she had acted contrary to her reason. And it was too late to draw back now, because he had straightened up and told her to follow his car.

When Leigh drew up outside the pub she had even bigger doubts about the wisdom of coming here. It wasn't very large, but was old and thatched and had ivy running up the walls. There were several expensive cars already in the car park, and Leigh guessed that the prices on the menu would be correspondingly high, and she just couldn't afford to waste any money on a lavish meal. So she drew back when Bryce came to escort her inside. He, however, mistook her hesitation and, glancing down at her skirt and jacket, said, 'You don't have to worry; this isn't a dressy place,' then put a firm hand under her elbow and led her inside.

They were shown to a table next to a window overlooking a pleasant garden by the landlord himself, who greeted Bryce by name. It was a typical country pub with oak beams, a large inglenook fireplace and a collection of Toby jugs on various shelves round the room. Ordinarily, it was the sort of surroundings that Leigh enjoyed, but to be alone with her boss made her feel tense and on edge. Her knee accidentally touched his as he sat down and she quickly tucked her legs under her chair, her heart starting to beat too rapidly.

'Do you come here a lot?' she asked, for something to say.

'Quite often. Mostly on a Sunday because it's the only place open apart from the Chinese and Indian restaurants in Shepton. I can't stand those.'

Leigh grimaced mirthlessly, recalling how she'd been living off Chinese food all week. She hadn't found the Indian restaurant yet; maybe she'd look for it tomorrow and live off curry next week instead of sweet and sour.

'What's so funny?' Bryce demanded, and Leigh looked up to find him watching her narrowly.

'Oh, nothing. Private joke.'

'Really?' His lips thinned and he suddenly seemed more cold and remote even than when he was ticking her off about something.

Luckily the waitress came along then and handed

them the menus so that Leigh could bury her head in hers, although she noticed that Bryce hardly seemed to glance at his before making up his mind. She was right, the dishes were expensive. They also sounded deliciously appetising and Leigh's stomach made hungry noises. But she determinedly chose just soup and the cheapest main course.

'Are you sure that's all you want?' Bryce asked in surprise.

'Yes, thank you.'

'You don't eat enough to keep a bird alive,' he commented. 'What would you like for an aperitif?'

'Nothing, thank you.'

A grim look came into Bryce's eyes and he said, 'Look, this isn't some sort of test. I know that you're flying tomorrow, but a couple of drinks now won't affect you.'

'All right, I'll have a gin and tonic, please.'

The waitress went away and Leigh made a business of getting her handkerchief out of her bag. When the drinks came Bryce lifted his and said, 'Cheers,' then touched his glass to hers. Their eyes met over the clinking glasses and Leigh hastily took a long drink, her throat feeling suddenly dry. For the first time she began to wonder just why he *had* asked her along. It certainly wasn't out of the goodness of his heart, because he hadn't got one, she decided cynically. And it wasn't to get to know her better as one of his employees, because he'd made it quite clear that he didn't intend her to be one for very long. So why?

'How do you find the hotel?'

Bryce's question interrupted her thoughts and

she gave him a non-committal answer. There was no point in telling him that she hated the place, that having to live there only added to the general misery of working at a job where you weren't wanted.

'Do you live near here?' she asked him, to fill the gap of silence.

'At Shepton Ferrers. I have a bachelor flat in one of those blocks that you pass going into the airport.'

'They look very . . .' Leigh hesitated as she remembered the glassed and balconied buildings, '. . . very modern,' she finished lamely.

His lips twisted into a mocking grin. 'I believe the word you want is utilitarian. They're nothing to look at, but they serve their purpose. And they're close to the airport so that I can get out there quickly if there's ever an emergency.'

'Does that often happen—an emergency, I mean?'

'No, only a couple of times. Once someone tried to break in and steal one of the planes, and another time there was a fire in one of the workshops at the airport and everyone was called out to move their planes out of the way in case the lot went up. But that was some time ago. We've never had an emergency with one of the planes, if that's what you were thinking.'

'No, I know.' He looked at her enquiringly, and Leigh admitted, 'I looked up your safety record before I accepted your offer of a job.'

'Did you?' Bryce sat back, looking at her over his glass as he took a drink, and Leigh raised her chin defiantly, feeling as if she'd been caught out in something. A strange look that she couldn't fathom came into his eyes for an instant and was as quickly gone. 'Very wise,' he remarked, as he set down his glass. 'It always pays to do your home-work.'

'But in this case I didn't do it thoroughly enough, did I?'

'In what way?'

'I didn't find out that Allerton's was run by a misogynist. If I had done it would have saved us both a lot of trouble.'

He laughed then, with genuine amusement. 'Oh, I'm no woman-hater, Leigh. Quite the opposite.'

It was a good job the waitress arrived with their food then, because Leigh could never have found a follow-up to that remark. And it wasn't only his words that had unnerved her. When he'd laughed his whole manner seemed to change so that it was like coming face to face with a stranger—and an extremely macho and attractive one at that. When he'd been cold and aggressive Leigh had been able to forget that he was a good-looking male, bury it under the dislike and antagonism he aroused in her, but now it suddenly hit her and set her pulses racing.

He started to talk to her about her interests, but Leigh answered only stiltedly, feeling that he had some reason in bringing her here that she couldn't fathom, and reluctant to give herself away. Only when he spoke of flying did she relax a little and answer his questions more readily, but really he had learnt everything there was to know about her flying career from her records; it was an open book.

To get the conversation away from herself, Leigh

asked, 'Did you found Allerton's yourself?'

'No, it was my father. He was a pilot during the war and started the company immediately afterwards. But he died five years ago and I took over completely.'

'But you fly yourself? Didn't you say that you were a pilot?'

'Yes, I trained in the R.A.F. and then flew with B.A. until my father's health broke and I came here to help him.'

Leigh looked at him with quickened interest and grudging respect. If he'd flown with British Airways that must mean that he'd got his Airline Transport Pilot's Licence and was able to pilot the big jets carrying hundreds of passengers. It was an ambition that all pilots, including Leigh, sought to attain, but now that dream was for her an impossible one. When South-East Air folded she saw all her hopes of ever attaining that licence collapse; there were just too many trained pilots available for the big airlines to choose from.

'It seems to be a thriving company,' she remarked.

'We manage to keep our heads above water,' Bryce conceded, then deliberately changed the subject. 'I hope you like this wine.'

'Thank you.' Leigh picked up the glass he'd filled for her, sniffed it and took a sip. 'Yes, it's fine.'

'Your sense of smell seems to have come back,' Bryce remarked dryly.

'What?' For a minute Leigh couldn't think what he was talking about, then remembered and smiled ruefully. 'Yes, just in time for the vegetable run next week.'

As she said it an idea occurred to her. Had he brought her here to tell her that he was getting rid of her and the meal was to soften the blow? But she almost laughed aloud at the thought; if Bryce Allerton was going to give her the sack he wouldn't attempt to be kind or tactful about it; he'd just tell her to get the hell out and enjoy doing it. So why? she wondered yet again. What possible reason could he have for bringing her here?

She refused a pudding and settled for a cup of coffee, mentally adding up the cost of her meal and wondering what she could possibly cut down on to pay for it.

When the waitress brought the bill Leigh immediately picked up her bag and said, 'We'll go halves, shall we?'

A surprised look came into his eyes. 'Certainly not. You're my guest.'

'Thanks, but I'd rather pay my share.' She took her purse out of her handbag. 'How much is it?'

'Put that away. I invited you here.'

'Not as I understood it,' Leigh pursued doggedly. 'You just told me that you could eat here and . . .'

'Leigh,' Bryce broke in menacingly, 'just do as you're told. If it makes you any happier, I'll put it down to expenses.'

She flushed a little but capitulated to his stronger will-power. 'All right. Thanks.' Excusing herself, she went into the cloakroom to apply fresh lipstick, wishing that she'd known he was going to pay so that she could have had more to eat. Immediately she hated herself for being so mercenary, even with Bryce Allerton who, she presumed, could well afford to take a girl out and give her a good time. But she'd never been out with a man just for a meal ticket and she didn't intend to start now. Not that this was like a real date, of course. She had automatically begun to tidy her hair, but now her hand slowed as she gazed at her reflection in the mirror. No, this wasn't a date, definitely not. They had both needed to eat, Bryce had suggested a convenient place, and had then insisted on paying because it would be an outrage to his masculine pride for any woman he was with to pay for herself. It was really nothing more than that. And yet tonight, for the first time, he'd called her by her Christian name. Surely that must mean something! Perhaps even that he was relenting towards her and might let her keep the job, she thought hopefully. This meal might even be his way of admitting that he'd been mistaken about her; a sort of peace offering. It wouldn't, she decided, be a form of apology, because somehow she could never imagine Bryce Allerton admitting that he was wrong to anyone.

He was waiting for her in the lobby, smoking a cigarette and leaning nonchalantly against the wall. When they went outside the air was still quite warm, the evening not yet dark.

'I could do with a walk after that meal,' Bryce remarked. 'Let's take a stroll round the village, shall we? It has all the ingredients of a typical English film scene.'

'What are those?' Leigh asked, more relaxed now that she thought she'd worked out his motive in bringing her here, especially as she had decided optimistically in her own favour.

'Oh, a de rigueur setting with thatched cottages clustered round a village green. A duckpond on the green and a wooden bench in the shade of ancient oak trees. And an equally ancient church with a spire reaching into the sky.'

He had begun to stroll along the road and Leigh fell into step beside him.

'You sound as if you're running it down. Don't you like the country?'

'Oh, sure. It's fine to live in if you've got a wife and kids, but there's not much point if you're on your own.'

'I don't agree with you. I think your surroundings are very important. And I love the country; I've lived in it all my life.'

'Ah, yes, you're from Devon, aren't you? You don't have an accent.'

'No, but I be able to speak with a Devon burr when I want to, zur,' she replied, stressing the heavy West Country dialect.

Bryce laughed and his footsteps slowed. They had come to his typical village green and they stopped for Leigh to look around. The sun was setting over the humped roofs of the cottages, sending long shadows across the neat gardens, already full of flowers. A young couple, their arms round each other's waist, passed them and turned into one of the smallest houses, closing the door firmly behind them. Leigh had a sudden longing to live in one of the cottages, to be part of such a small, compact community, where everyone is dependent upon, and important to, everyone else. She remembered her bleak hotel room and turned abruptly away. 'We'd better be getting back.'

'But there's a view you'll probably enjoy just down this lane.'

Without waiting for her to agree, Bryce led her along a narrow lane between the cottages for a hundred yards or so, then stopped at a stile beyond which a path led upwards through some trees to the ridge of a hill.

'Here, I'll give you a hand.' Bryce climbed over the stile and held out his hand.

Leigh hesitated on the other side. 'It will be too dark to see anything, won't it?'

'Not if we hurry. Come along.'

He spoke so imperiously that Leigh found herself obeying him. She gave him her hand and he helped her to jump lightly down. But then he kept hold of her arm.

'I can manage, thanks,' she assured him, trying to withdraw it.

'Nonsense, you'll probably catch your heel in a rabbit hole and break your ankle or something.' And he kept a firm hold.

The path was short but quite steep, and Leigh was panting a little as they emerged from the trees to the top of the ridge. But it was well worth the climb. The village lay spread out before them and beyond it the rolling countryside, freshly ploughed and planted, ready for the new harvest. As they watched the sun slowly sank down out of sight, the last rays licking the fields until they too slowly disappeared from view as if reluctant to leave the fertile land.

Leigh sighed and stirred. 'How wonderful to be able to see a sight like that every day of your life!' Bryce didn't answer and she became aware that he was still holding her arm. 'Bryce?' she said uncertainly.

He didn't say anything, just turned her round, then pulled her into his arms and kissed her. It happened so suddenly that Leigh was completely unprepared. Her lips were soft and yielding as his mouth came down on hers, and for a moment she was too surprised to react. Then she made a sound of protest and tried to pull away, but his arms tightened, holding her against him. His lips were hard and insinuatingly insistent, trying to make her open her mouth and respond to him. Leigh's hands went up to his shoulders to push him away, but somehow they just rested there instead as he held her closer.

'Relax,' he murmured against her mouth. 'Just relax.'

His lips moved over hers in little exploratory kisses and then, almost against her will, Leigh's mouth opened a little and she began to respond, losing herself in the warmth of his embrace, in the sensations his kiss aroused in her. Immediately Bryce became more importuning, so that a tremor of awareness ran through her body. He felt it, he couldn't help but feel it, and his right hand slid down to her hips, pressing her against him as he kissed her with growing passion. He wound a hand in the thickness of her hair and she lifted her chin so that his lips could explore the line of her neck and gently bite her ear before returning hungrily to her mouth.

When he at last lifted his head, Leigh was trembling and her legs felt strangely weak at the knees. Bryce's voice, too, sounded thick and unsteady as he said, 'Why don't we continue this somewhere more comfortable?'

Feeling slightly dazed and not really taking in what he was saying, Leigh murmured, 'What do you mean?'

Bryce was still holding her and he again bent his head to nuzzle her ear, at the same time pulling her close against him. 'Let's go back to my place,' he suggested.

The things he was doing to her ear were sending her crazy, but the hardness of his body left her in no doubt of his intentions, and she quickly stepped out of his arms. 'Hey, you're going too fast for me!'

Immediately he reached for her again, but she held him off. 'Stop playing games,' he muttered, his brows drawing into a frown.

'I'm not. Bryce, I hardly know you.'

'What's there to know—except that you want me as much as I want you?'

He caught her wrist, jerking her forward so that she lost her balance and stumbled towards him. Immediately his arms went round her, pinning her against him as his mouth came down on hers, demanding a response. Leigh managed to resist for a few moments, but then capitulated to the heady emotions he was arousing, her hands going up round his neck and her mouth opening submissively.

'Come on. Let's go.' He took hold of her hand to lead her down the now darkened path, but Leigh drew back, afraid of her own emotions and of being rushed into something she wasn't sure she wanted. Or at least what her reason told her she ought not to want; because her body definitely did, it was on fire with awareness and need, craving the pleasure and fulfilment that only a man's love could give.

'Wait,' she stammered. 'I—I'm not sure.'

Bryce turned towards her and laughed harshly. 'I told you not to play games with me. You knew I'd lead up to this from the moment I asked you to have dinner with me.'

Leigh stared at him, feeling suddenly sick. It was almost dark now, but there was just enough light for her to make out the look of derision on his face. So now she knew why he'd brought her here; he'd thought her cheap and available, that one meal would buy his way into bed with her! The thought made her so angry that she didn't even think about the consequences before she lifted her hand to hit him across the face.

His reaction was instantaneous. He certainly couldn't have anticipated her action in the gloom, but his hand shot up and caught her wrist, and at the same time he jerked his head back so that she missed him completely. 'What the hell . . .'

'You louse! You pig! How *dare* you? Do you expect every girl you take out for a meal to pay for it by going back to your flat with you?' Angrily she jerked her wrist from his hold and started to hurry down the path back towards the road.

Bryce caught her up and put a hand under her arm, stopping her. 'You'll break your neck if you try to run down here.'

'Let go of me, damn you. You arrogant, conceited swine!'

His grip tightened on her elbow, hurting her. 'You were willing enough when I kissed you.'

That what he'd said was true only inflamed

Leigh's anger. 'Just what kind of a man are you?' she demanded furiously. 'You treat me like dirt, tell me that you're going to get rid of me just as soon as you can, and then expect me to fall into your bed the first time you make a pass!' A thought occurred to her that made her gasp. 'Or is going to bed with you a condition of keeping my job? Is that it? If I let you make love to me you'll let me stay on at Allerton's?'

For a moment he stood silently, just staring at her, then he said slowly, 'What would your answer be if I said it was?'

'I'd say keep your job,' Leigh retorted at once. 'And you can just go to hell, Bryce Allerton! I was right about you the first time I met you. I thought then that you were nothing but a womaniser. Only I didn't know just how low you'd stoop to . . .'

She broke off abruptly as Bryce grabbed her other arm and shook her angrily. 'Have you finished?'

'No, I haven't. I think you're nothing but a . . .'

His hand came up suddenly and gripped her throat, so that she stopped abruptly. 'I've had about as much as I'm going to take from you, young lady. So just shut up, will you?'

He looked so angry that awareness of her surroundings at last broke through her own fury. Leigh nodded slowly and Bryce took away his hand. 'All right. Now, let's walk down to the road.' This time when he took her arm she didn't try to stop him, and she did in fact stumble a couple of times on the uneven ground, but only because she was still so mad. When they reached the road he immediately let her go, before she had the satisfaction of telling him to, and she walked quickly back the way they'd come. Bryce strode easily along beside her, having no trouble in keeping pace and making no attempt to speak to her.

When they reached the car park beside the pub, Leigh turned and said stiffly, 'I shall call at Allerton's at ten o'clock tomorrow morning. Will you please have my insurance cards and my wages ready for me to collect?'

Bryce took his car keys out of his pocket and unlocked the door of his car before he turned to look at her. 'No, I won't,' he replied deliberately. 'You'll come to the airport tomorrow morning in time to take the vegetable run again.'

Leigh stared at him incredulously. 'Are you crazy? If you think I'd work for you after tonight, then . . .'

'You'll be there,' Bryce broke in. 'Because you need this job, need it badly. And just for the moment I need you.' He moved a little so that the light on the wall threw a dark, satanic shadow across his face. 'And besides,' he added menacingly, 'we both know it isn't over between us. You want me as much as I want you. And I'm going to take you to bed before we're through.'

CHAPTER FOUR

LEIGH parked the Mini outside Allerton's the next morning and got slowly out of the car. The outside air felt chilly and she hugged her coat round her. There was only one other car in the car park, and she gave a small sigh of relief when she saw that it wasn't Bryce's Jaguar. If it had been, she knew that she would have turned the car round and driven right back to the hotel. Because it was only five-fifteen and she was turning up to take the vegetable run just as Bryce had predicted. Or perhaps ordered would be a better word, she thought wryly as she walked round to the airfield side of the building. Not that coming here had been an easy decision. She had lain awake a long time last night after she had left him outside the pub and driven back to her hotel. Pride had wrestled with realism, but in the end it had come down to the basic question of economics; she just couldn't afford to walk out of the job, even if it only went on until the end of her month's trial. Another three weeks' wages would at least enable her to pay back the money she'd borrowed from her parents and the sum she owed on the Tiger Moth. It would even give her some to live on while she looked round for another job. Only Leigh doubted very much whether she would be able to get another flying job, those were very thin on the ground these days.

She greeted Vic Parker who was getting the plane

ready in the hangar, then went into the crew room
to phone the control tower and get the latest
weather report and wind strengths so that she
could work out her flight plan and approximate
E.T.A.s. When she came out the plane was on the
tarmac waiting for her and Leigh went towards it
eagerly; when there was a prospect of not being
able to fly at all, even the onion run was to be
enjoyed.

The day went off uneventfully, as did the next.
She didn't see Bryce and certainly didn't seek him
out. On the Wednesday her name was down on the
roster to do two runs: one in the morning and one
in the afternoon, with a couple of hours' wait in
between. Don Chapman happened to be there at
the same time and he made her go out with him to
a small restaurant in the town where he bought her
lunch.

'How's it going?' he asked her as he watched her
tuck into a large steak and kidney pudding.

'Oh, fine,' Leigh lied heartily. 'Do you live near
here, Don?'

'Don't change the subject. What's the hotel
like?'

'Very good.'

His eyebrows rose in disbelief. 'You seem to
forget that I spent the greater part of my life in
hotel rooms when I was flying with B.A., and I've
never found one yet that was very good. They're
all too impersonal when you're on your own and
you're just using the place as a dormitory. Now,
what's it really like?'

Leigh lowered her fork to study his face, noting
the friendly twinkle in his eyes and remembering

that he had grown-up children of his own. 'It's awful,' she confided. 'I hate it.'

'Why don't you try and find something else?'

'I've looked, but there's nothing much available—not that I can afford, anyway.'

Don looked at her shrewdly. 'You were out of work before you came here, weren't you?'

'Yes, for several months.'

'And you don't get paid until the end of the month.'

'If I last that long,' Leigh answered bitterly. 'The way it looks at the moment, Bryce could give me the sack any day.'

'No, he won't,' Don said unexpectedly. 'He needs you.'

Leigh looked at him in surprise, remembering that Bryce had said much the same thing on Sunday night. 'He does? He certainly didn't give me that impression when I arrived here.'

Don laughed. 'No, I don't suppose he did. I've never seen him so mad as when he found out you were a girl. He doesn't like to be made to look a fool, does Bryce.'

'But why does he need me?'

'Because he's a pilot short, of course. And also because he's just won a contract with a local car manufacturers to ferry their executives, technicians and salesmen all over Britain and Europe. That contract starts on the first of May and Bryce is getting a new plane on the strength of it; a Piper Navajo Chieftain. Mike Stewart is going to take over that plane, so Bryce wanted a pilot to take over Mike's work, but he also needed one to replace a chap who walked out about three weeks ago. The one whose place you took.'

'So that's why he wanted someone at such short notice.'

'Mm. And why he didn't give himself time to check your record thoroughly enough to find out you were a female of the species,' Don added with a chuckle.

'Well, he won't find it difficult to replace me,' Leigh observed pessimistically. 'There are a lot of good pilots looking for jobs.'

'Not as many as you think. A lot of them take early retirement, others get good redundancy payments and start up businesses of their own. And anyway, Bryce would be a fool to replace you. You handle a plane well, your times are good, and you're light on repairs.'

Stupid tears prickled Leigh's eyes at his kindness and her voice was husky as she said, 'Thanks, Don. You've no idea how I needed that.'

'Nonsense,' he replied gruffly. 'You don't need me to tell you you're a good pilot. And Bryce doesn't need me to tell him either, though I will, of course.'

'It wouldn't make any difference; he wants me out. He'll get rid of me as soon as he can find someone else.'

'Then he'll be a fool. But in the meantime we must try and find you somewhere more congenial to live.' Don got out his pipe and lit it. 'Now,' he went on when the pipe was glowing nicely, 'my son owns a small cottage—a very small cottage—in a village near here. At the moment he's working in America and will be for the next three months, so I'm keeping an eye on the place for him. So it would do me a good turn if you'd care to move in and look after it, keep the garden tidy and so on.'

Leigh looked at him speechlessly for a moment, then said hastily, 'Oh, it sounds wonderful. How much rent would you want?'

'Well, as you'd be a sort of caretaker I think we can waive the rent. As I said, you'd be doing me a favour.'

'That's very kind of you, Don, and I really appreciate it, but I couldn't take it unless I paid you some rent,' Leigh said firmly.

Don studied her face for a moment, working out whether that was just a token gesture, decided it wasn't and nodded. 'All right, we'll say fifteen pounds a week, then. But you'd better have a look at the place and make sure you like it before you come to any decision.'

'When?' Leigh asked eagerly.

He smiled through the pipe smoke. 'How about this evening? I'll write down the address for you and I'll meet you there tonight at seven. That suit you?'

'Fine.' He noted down the address and gave it to her. 'Oh, but I know where this is,' Leigh exclaimed. 'I went to that village when I first came here. It's a pretty little place.'

They talked a little longer, then left to go back to work. As they were driving back, a thought occurred to Leigh and she asked, 'By the way, why did the pilot I'm replacing walk out?'

Don was silent for a moment, then said in a tone of some embarrassment, 'There was some trouble with his wife. The usual thing, an extra-marital affair. She came down to the airport a couple of times and there was an almighty row between the three of them.'

'The three of them?'

'The pilot and his wife and Bryce Allerton. And it ended with the pilot leaving there and then. Though whether he left or Bryce sacked him, I don't know. They've moved away now, I hear—gone up north somewhere. Good thing, if they manage to patch things up, but I doubt it; it had gone too far.'

'Yes, I see,' Leigh said hollowly. She would have liked to ask Don more, but they were turning into the airport and the opportunity was lost. So Bryce had been having an affair with the wife of one of his own pilots, had he? The information should hardly have surprised her, not after Sunday night, but somehow it did. She *knew* he was a skunk from the way he'd tried to blackmail her into giving herself to him in exchange for keeping her job, and yet he had had such a devastating effect on her sexually that she wanted to believe better of him. Naturally she had thought about that parting taunt he had made, thought about it more than once, but she had put it down to bravado on his part, a determination to have the last word. But it didn't do to think about Sunday night, not now that she had had confirmation of the type of man he was.

That afternoon she flew a cargo of freight up to Birmingham, where she picked up another load and took it across country to Rhoose airport near Cardiff. When she got back she was surprised to find all four of the other pilots standing around on the tarmac outside the crew room.

'Bryce is bringing in the new Piper Navajo

today,' Mike Stewart told her. 'He should be here any minute.'

She turned and waited with them, talking about planes they'd flown, those that were good, those that had been pigs to handle, about stalls and spins and side-slips. The sort of talk that always arose when groups of fliers got together, talk that cut across all barriers of age, race, and even sex. For those few minutes Leigh was one of them, and she felt at ease for the first time since she had been working for Allerton's. Then they heard the noise of an engine and all looked up to see the Navajo dropping down through the white, billowing clouds to circle the airfield and come into the wind. The plane, with its turquoise and white markings and the distinctive AAC logo on the tail, looking beautiful as the sun caught it and reflected off the wings. Bryce brought it down precisely and steadily to land on the runway like a whisper on a lake. He taxied over to the hangar and switched off the engine. A beautiful plane, and a beautiful landing, Leigh had to admit.

The others all went over to look at the plane, but Leigh had no wish to meet Bryce and went back into the crew room to do her paperwork. After a quarter of an hour or so Don and the other two pilots came back and went off home, then Mike and Bryce came in together, discussing the new plane and the test flight they intended to give it the next day. Leigh hastily finished writing and stood up as they came in, collecting her things together so that she could leave.

But Mike stopped her. 'What do you think of the Navajo?' he asked her.

'It looks beautiful, you must be looking forward to flying her.'

'Have you flown one before?'

Leigh shook her head. 'No. Well, I must be off.' She was very aware of Bryce standing in the room a few feet behind Mike, but so far she had kept her attention on putting her things back in her flight bag and had managed to avoid meeting his eyes. She started to move towards the door, but Mike put a restraining hand on her arm.

'How about coming out for a drink to celebrate getting the new plane?'

'Sorry, Mike, I'm busy tonight.'

'Got a date?'

Leigh was about to explain that she was meeting Don, but she heard Bryce make a small, sneering sound and she turned to look at him. His eyes held hers, cold and challenging, and Leigh's chin came up defiantly. 'Yes, as a matter of fact I have.'

She saw the look in his eyes begin to change to a frown, but then she coolly nodded goodnight to Mike, turned, and left.

The cottage was everything she could possibly have hoped for. It was very small, admittedly; situated in a terraced row that had tiny gardens fronting on to the road that ran through the village of Little Marsden. It was an old village, strung out on the sides of the road with one or two little shops and a pub, all the roofs sagging under the weight of age, with no new houses to spoil the look of the place. Don's son's cottage was the third one along in the terrace with sash windows giving light to just two rooms upstairs and two down. You opened the white-painted front door and stepped down into the living room which had an old-fashioned fireplace with an ornate metal surround and a door which gave on to a twisting staircase to the upper rooms. Not much had been done to this room except to furnish it with a small settee and a few other pieces of furniture, but the back room had been made into an up-to-date country kitchen with pine units, a Welsh dresser and a dining table and chairs, again in pine. Upstairs, the front room contained only a big double bed, a wardrobe and a dressing-table, but the back room had been made into a very practical bathroom. The decor and furniture were a bit too masculine and austere for Leigh's taste, but she certainly wasn't going to quibble about that.

'Come and see the garden,' Don suggested, and led her out of the back door. The garden was only the width of the house but was quite long, mainly laid to lawn, but dotted with fruit trees that were beginning to bud. Nearer the house was a patio area, that was screened from the neighbouring houses, where Don said that his son had used to hold barbecue parties.

'Oh, Don, it's exactly what I wanted,' Leigh exclaimed. 'Are you sure your son won't mind me living here?'

'Quite sure,' Don stated with complete disregard for his son's feelings. 'He'll be glad to have it occupied. And now that we don't have the worry of looking after the cottage, my wife and I can take the opportunity to go to America to visit him. And besides, you need to get out of that hotel. I've noticed that you're looking a little peaky this week.'

'I'm very grateful, Don. I really am,' Leigh told him earnestly.

'Nonsense,' he returned gruffly. 'When would you like to move in?'

'Well . . . tomorrow, if that's okay with you.'

'That's fine. Here are the keys. Now, my wife's got dinner waiting for us both.'

'Oh, but I couldn't put you to that much trouble. You've been kind enough already,' Leigh protested.

'But I've promised her that I'll bring you. And she'd never forgive me if I didn't. She's dying of curiosity, you see. Can't wait to meet the girl who put one over on Bryce,' Don confided.

So Leigh laughed and capitulated and had the most pleasant evening she had spent in quite some time. The next morning she packed all her belongings into the Mini and checked out of the Beechwood Hotel, leaving her things in the car while she was working. Today she had dressed smartly because she'd been given a taxi run. It would normally have been Mike's job, but he and Bryce were happily playing with the new plane, so she had been given the Aztec to take to Cambridge to collect some jockeys and trainers and fly them to the races at Haydock Park, roughly midway between Manchester and Liverpool.

She arrived at Cambridge well on time and parked on the apron while she went to the control office for the routine report after landing. They told her where to find her passengers and Leigh went into the passenger reception area to look for them. There were five of them, four men and a woman. Two of the men, from their size and youth, were obviously jockeys, and the other two must both be trainers, one of whom, Leigh noted from her passenger list, had brought along his wife.

Dressed in her navy pleated skirt and jacket, her hair shining like a new chestnut, Leigh went up to them and said politely, 'Good morning. I believe you're the party for Haydock who've chartered a plane from Allerton's?' They all made assenting noises and Leigh smiled. 'The plane's waiting. Would you follow me, please?'

'Don't tell me Allerton's are giving us stewardess service on their planes now,' one of the jockeys remarked as he fell into step beside her. 'If you guarantee to be on all their flights, darlin',' then I'll guarantee to use them every time!'

'Sorry, I'm afraid they don't run to serving meals and drinks on board,' Leigh replied as they came to the plane. 'If you'll give me your saddles and bags I'll stow them in the luggage compartment.'

But the two jockeys wouldn't let her. 'A slip of a thing like you would buckle under the weight of our stuff,' one told her, and they insisted on putting their things in the hold themselves. Leigh tried not to look amused at being called a slip of a thing by a man who probably weighed about the same as she did and was a whole head shorter.

The jockeys got into the back seat and the older trainer and his wife in the middle, which left only the other man, who was in his early forties, waiting for the pilot to arrive so that he could get into the right-hand seat. Leigh gave him a polite smile, climbed into the cockpit and sat in the pilot seat, trying to ignore the thunderstruck looks on the faces of her passengers.

'Oh, my God,' she heard one of the jockeys moan faintly. 'She's flying the plane!'

The other man climbed in beside her and Leigh made sure the door was secured and they had their straps on, then hastily put on the headphones and asked for clearance before one of them changed their minds and asked to get out. She had flown passengers loads of times before, of course, but not in such close contact. In her old job the passengers usually didn't even find out that the co-pilot was a girl, or if they did they were usually already in the air and couldn't do much about it. Although why they had this basic assumption that a woman couldn't handle a plane as well as a man, Leigh failed to see. Once their reaction would have angered her, but now she was immune to it and just hoped that it wouldn't put them off using Allerton's again.

For this reason she flew them as steadily as she knew how and eventually was pleased to hear them relax as they started to chat to each other. Leigh listened idly when she wasn't speaking over the radio, and gathered that she had been mistaken; the man sitting next to her wasn't a trainer but an owner with several racehorses. From the deferential way the others spoke to him he must have been quite important or very rich, perhaps both, but Leigh had never heard of him before, but then she knew little about the worlds of either high finance or racing.

There was a runway adjoining the racecourse at Haydock Park and Leigh brought the Aztec in to

land and gently roll across the grass, even though
it was raining quite hard. She parked the plane in
a line of others, either air charter or private, and
settled down to read a book to while away the long
afternoon of waiting until the last race was run at
five o'clock. After a couple of hours, however,
someone banged on the side of the plane and Leigh
opened the door to find a man in a waiter's jacket
holding a covered tray out to her. 'Mr Hollander
sent this along for you.'

Leigh recognised the name as that of the passenger who had sat beside her, so she took the tray.
Under the cover, she was amazed to find a plate of
smoked salmon sandwiches, a dish of strawberries
and cream and a bottle of fruit juice with a glass.
She gazed at the food in some astonishment, then
burst out laughing; evidently her passenger also
thought that she was too frail to fly the plane and
was determined to build her up before the return
journey!

When the passengers returned around a quarter
to six, Leigh thanked Mr Hollander politely for his
kind gesture, but he merely nodded and gave his
attention to the others as they discussed the day's
racing. Mr Hollander, it seemed, had had a lucky
day; one of his horses had won and another had
come second. Perhaps it was because of this that
he pressed a banknote into her hand as he left.
Leigh tried to give it back, but he got out of the
plane first and she had to wait until the others had
all disembarked before she could herself get out to
follow him, but then the jockeys wanted their
saddles and holdalls out of the baggage compartment, so Leigh had to shove the note in her pocket

to leave her hands free, and by the time she had finished Mr Hollander had gone.

She was rather worried about it, not knowing what the company's policy was regarding tips; she had never been offered one before and it hadn't occurred to her to ask. When she got back in the plane and took the note out of her pocket, she was even more worried—it was for twenty pounds!

That evening, she moved into the cottage. It didn't take long, she didn't have that much with her. Really all she had to do was to move the clothes that her absent landlord had left behind to one end of the wardrobe and hang her own beside them. But she felt a great sense of satisfaction as she picked flowers out of the garden and put them into every room, stuck in any container she could find; Don's son didn't seem to go in for vases. And when it grew dark she lit the fire in the living-room and sat on the floor in front of it, a mug of coffee in her hands as she watched the flickering flames. It was much, much better than the hotel and she felt far more content, but even so her thoughts kept going back to Bryce Allerton as she wondered when he would make his next move against her. That he would make a move Leigh was in no doubt; he just wasn't the kind of man to let the situation hang fire. One way or another he was bound to do something soon. Leigh shivered, remembering the experienced way he had kissed her, and fervently hoped his attack wouldn't be in that direction again, because she just didn't know if she could handle it.

Fate played tricks on her the next morning, the bad things happening in threes, as they usually do.

First her alarm clock failed to go off because the battery had given out, so she got up late, and had to go without breakfast, then she had to queue for petrol so that she was nearly late for work, and thirdly as she dashed into the reception area to collect the day's work schedule she ran straight into Bryce. Literally into him. He had to put his arms out and catch her to stop them both from over-balancing.

'Oops, sorry!' Leigh made the apology before she looked up. 'Oh, it's you!'

'As you say.' Bryce looked down at her unsmilingly, his face almost stern, then his arms tightened and he bent to kiss her. 'You're late,' he added as if nothing had happened, when he raised his head a minute later.

'No, I'm not, I'm dead on time,' Leigh replied in an unsteady tone, making no move to get away as his mouth came down to find hers again.

Behind them, the front door of the building rattled and a cold rush of air signalled someone's arrival, and Bryce unhurriedly stepped back and moved away. 'Morning, Carol.'

Leigh's nerves were jumping and she had to collect herself for a minute before she could turn round. Bryce was standing at the reception desk going through the pile of post, apparently quite unperturbed. Carol gave Leigh a funny, suspicious kind of look, as well she might, and handed her the papers she would need for the cargo she was collecting and delivering that day. Leigh went to hurry out to the crew room to file her flight plan, but Bryce stopped her. 'Can you work over the weekend?'

Leigh hesitated; this weekend had an extra day because it included the national May Day bank holiday on Monday, and ordinarily she would have visited her parents, but she had only been away for a couple of weeks so there was no great urgency to go back yet. Coming to a swift decision, she answered, 'I can work on Saturday and Sunday, but not Monday.'

'Fair enough. Come and see me when you get back this afternoon and I'll give you the schedule.'

Leigh nodded and hurried away to work out her flight plan. There was no interesting taxi-work to do today, just a routine cargo flight to Southend and then up to Sheffield, stopping at Birmingham on the way back. Mike passed her on the way out to the tarmac and tried to stop and say hello.

'Sorry, Mike, can't stop,' she called over her shoulder, and hurried out to the plane. After the pre-flight checks her luck seemed to change, because she was cleared for immediate take-off, taxiing towards the runway and waving back to Mike when she saw him come out of the crew room and raise his arms to her.

Today the weather, that all-important element to fliers, was clear and Leigh climbed steadily to three thousand, five hundred feet before levelling off, the sun streaming in the windows so brightly that she had to put on sunglasses. She settled back in her seat and flew on steadily, glad of a respite after the traumas of the morning, her thoughts free now to remember the casual way Bryce had kissed her, right there in the reception area. Had Carol seen? she wondered. Even if she hadn't, Carol must certainly have suspected something, from the odd way the other girl had looked at her. The louse! Leigh thought. Why did he have to go and kiss her there? And just why hadn't she resisted him instead of standing there like a stupid, dewy-eyed schoolgirl? she berated herself disgustedly. Anybody would think she was fifteen instead of twenty-five, the way she was behaving. And she still had to get through seeing him alone in his office tonight, when he told her what work he had for her over the weekend. Leigh wished, now, that she'd forgone the extra work rather than be alone with Bryce, but she crossly told herself not to be so stupid. All she had to do if he made any suggestions was to say no and keep saying no. But how to make it sound as if she meant it, an inner voice murmured, and what if Bryce wouldn't take no for an answer?

Her thoughts were rudely interrupted as her call sign came over the radio. 'Golf Bravo Delta Echo Sierra, this is Golf Bravo Bravo November Tango. Do you read me?'

'Roger, November Tango, go ahead, please.'

'November Tango, this is Delta Echo. Please change your frequency to one-two-five point two-five. Repeat, please change your frequency to one-two-five point two-five.'

Mystified, Leigh reached up to the console of instruments above the windscreen and twisted the knobs to the new frequency, an unusual one that was seldom used by commercial aircraft. Immediately she had done so she spoke into the headset. 'Hallo, Delta Echo, this is November Tango. Are you receiving me?'

'Loud and clear, November Tango.' Then the

formal voice changed. 'Leigh, this is Mike. Have you looked at your collection and delivery notes? You've picked up the wrong ones.'

'What?' Hastily Leigh put the plane on auto-pilot and picked up the clipboard that she always used to attach the notes to. A hasty flip through confirmed the bad news. 'Oh, no! I've got yours.'

'That's right. We'll have to land somewhere and swap them over.'

'Where are you?' Leigh asked him hopefully.

'Right behind you. I tried to stop you as you were about to take off, but I was just too late.'

'Oh, hell, what a mix-up! You've had time to think—where do you suggest we land?'

'I think our best bet would be Elstree,' he replied, naming a small airfield in Hertfordshire. 'You go in first and wait. I should be about a quarter of an hour after you.'

Leigh looked again at the first heading on Mike's list. 'But you're supposed to be going to Newcastle. Mike, it's miles out of your way!'

'Can't be helped. And anyway, I've got the faster plane; I'll be able to make up some of the time, and I can always make an excuse to cover the delay. Don't worry,' he added with a chuckle, 'we won't let Bryce find out.'

'Thanks, Mike,' Leigh said fervently, imagining just what would happen if Bryce *did* find out. 'I'll switch back to the other frequency and see you at Elstree.'

She was waiting anxiously by the taxiway and ran over to him as soon as he landed and came to a standstill, the wrong notes in her hand. Mike swung open his door and jumped to the ground.

'Here you are,' he said, passing over the other notes with a grin. 'Make sure you look at them next time before you pick them up!'

'I didn't pick them up, they were handed to me. But I should still have checked. Thanks, Mike,' she added gratefully. 'I don't know what I would have done if I'd got all the way to Southend before I found out. What a pity I didn't realise you were trying to attract my attention instead of just waving.'

'Never mind, no harm done as long as Bryce doesn't find out.'

'You'll be wanting to get off so that you can make up time. Thanks again for coming after me, Mike.'

She went to move away, but Mike said, 'What about the landing fees here? We don't want them sending in the bill to Allerton's.'

'It's okay, I paid for both of us when I reported to the control office.'

'Good.' But he didn't seem to be in any hurry to go. 'How about coming out for a drink after work to start off the long weekend?'

'I'm sorry, Mike, I can't.'

'Another date?'

'No. Bryce wants to see me when I get back today.'

'Well, that won't take too long, will it? We could go for a drink afterwards.' Leigh hesitated, and he added with a crooked grin, 'I do deserve some reward for getting you out of trouble, don't I?'

'Yes, of course.' But Leigh said it uncertainly, realising that she was being coerced into doing something she didn't really want to. 'Just for a drink, then.'

'Great! I'll hang around in the crew room until you're through with Bryce. See you.' He climbed into the cockpit and gave her a wave as he started up the engines.

Leigh ran back to her own plane and followed him down to the runway, taking off two minutes later and turning in the opposite direction. Clipping the correct notes to her board, she cursed herself for not having checked them when Carol handed them to her. But then she remembered that she had been thoroughly kissed not two minutes earlier and wasn't surprised that she hadn't been functioning properly. But that was really no excuse; the very fact that Carol had bothered to give them to her should have alerted her, but the other girl had made no further trouble for her since the episode with the log books and Leigh had supposed that Bryce had realised she was to blame and given the girl a ticking off. But warned or not, Carol had tried to get her into trouble again. And it could have had disastrous results; Leigh grew cold as she thought what Bryce's reaction would have been if she'd wasted the time and petrol going to Southend and then coming back for the correct notes. He would have been livid, and justifiably too, because she really had no excuse; the responsibility was hers and hers alone. But thanks to Mike that calamity had been averted.

But now, Leigh thought ruefully, she was stuck with going out for a drink with Mike whether she liked it or not. And turning it over in her mind, she found that she wasn't particularly keen on the idea. She supposed Mike was nice enough, quite good-looking and presentable, so that there was

no exact reason she could put her finger on for not
wanting to go out with him, but she still felt reluctant to do so. Perhaps it was because he had been
that bit too eager, asking her out almost before
he'd met her properly and two or three times since,
so that she'd felt pressured into agreeing. And now
she had had no choice but to accept because he
had lost no time in pointing out that she owed it to
him. Well, he needn't think that her gratitude went
further than having a drink with him, Leigh
thought rather grimly. People had tried that angle
before, and she had learnt not to give in to blackmail, moral or otherwise.

She managed to make up the time that she had
lost during the day and landed back at Shepton
Ferrers about five in the afternoon. As she taxied
over to the hangar she noticed that Mike's plane
wasn't yet back, and she wondered rather anxiously
whether he would be very long in coming in. If he
was much later than usual Bryce would certainly
want to know why. She hung around for about ten
minutes, talking to Vic Parker about the plane, although there was nothing wrong with it, and then
began to walk slowly towards the crew room,
doubly reluctant to face Bryce now. But just as she
reached the door, the sound of an engine reached
her ears and she looked up to see Mike coming in
to land. So that was one load off her mind. Now
all she had to worry about was how to play it cool
with a man who could make her blood boil with
anger one minute and turn her to a quivering jelly
the next just by asserting his sexual masculinity.

Don Chapman and one of the other pilots were
already in the crew room and she chatted to them

for some minutes before sitting down to make up her logs. When Mike came in he immediately came over and leaned down close to speak to her, lowering his voice so that the others couldn't hear.

'Everything go okay?' he asked. 'No one's suspicious?'

'No, everything's fine,' Leigh replied in a normal voice, disliking his conspiratorial air and knowing that Don was looking over in surprise.

'Good. See you later.' Mike gave her a wink and straightened up, going over to the coffee machine.

After she'd finished writing, Leigh didn't hurry up to Bryce's office, instead she went into the ladies' loo and took her time over combing her hair and touching up her make-up. But then she realised that she was just hanging out the time and pulled herself together. She wasn't afraid of the man, was she? Who the hell did he think he was anyway—God's gift to women? Just because he was big and attractive and too damn masculine, it didn't mean that he could go around snapping his fingers at any woman he fancied and expect them just to fall into his arms, did it?

It took quite a bit of argument along those lines before Leigh had worked herself up into a sufficiently defiant mood in which to face Bryce. She looked at herself in the mirror and noticed that her cheeks were slightly flushed, her eyes bright and her chin determined. Without knowing why, her hand went to her mouth, touching her lips, recalling how it had felt when Bryce had kissed her. Opening her bag, she took out her precious French perfume and applied some to her neck and temples. Then she cursed herself roundly for a fool; the man was nothing more than a stud, and she certainly had no intention of adding to his list, so why bother to make herself more attractive for him? Glancing at her watch, she saw that she'd been in the cloakroom for almost twenty minutes. There could be no putting off the evil hour any longer; bracing her shoulders, Leigh walked out of the room and up to Bryce's office.

CHAPTER FIVE

IT was an anti-climax. Anything had to be, she supposed, after the way she'd built herself up to face him. Bryce was talking on the telephone and merely motioned her to a chair after she'd knocked and gone in. He was having an argument with someone about a delivery date, an argument which he won, of course. Leigh hadn't thought much before about how an air charter firm was run, but as she watched him she began to see just how much drive and energy he put into it to make it function so efficiently.

As he put the phone down Bryce ran a hand through his hair and sat back in his chair rather wearily. 'It's been one of those weeks,' he remarked. His grey eyes ran over her, noting how she was sitting upright on the edge of the chair, her hands folded tightly together in her lap. Getting up, he crossed over to a cabinet in the corner, poured out two gin and tonics and brought one over to her. 'Here.'

Leigh took the glass reluctantly; if he'd asked her if she wanted a drink she would have refused. But perhaps he knew that.

'How has your day gone?'

She looked at him warily, immediately afraid that he had somehow found out about the mix-up over the delivery notes and was trying to catch her out. But she didn't see how he could possibly know, so she said over-brightly, 'Oh, fine just fine.'

'Good.' He half sat on the edge of the desk nearest to her and turned to lean back over it as he selected a paper from a pile in his tray. 'Here's your schedule for the next two days. Tomorrow I want you to take a television crew over to France, wait for them and bring them back. They've assured me that they'll only take about four hours, but from previous experience with them you can bet your life they'll take six.' He noticed that Leigh was looking at him in surprise and said, 'That's okay, isn't it?'

'Yes, of course. It's just that . . .' she shrugged her shoulders, 'well, I didn't think you wanted me to do taxi work. I thought it was freight again.'

His eyes settled on her for a moment before he said shortly, 'There was no one else available to take them. And the same goes for the Sunday job. It's just for the afternoon, in case you have a long day on Saturday. Some people who have a boat-yard in the Isle of Wight want us to fly some prospective customers down there. The film crew you'll have to pick up at Gatwick, but you'll have to go to East Midlands Airport to pick up the people on Sunday. The times are all noted down,' he added, passing the schedule to her.

Leigh looked at it rather unseeingly, then finished her drink and stood up. I'll say goodnight, then.' She looked round for somewhere to put the glass, but there was only the desk. She crossed to it, put her glass down and went to move away. But Bryce caught her wrist. 'Don't be in so much of a hurry,' he said softly.

Leigh stood still, not speaking, but her heart

gave a queer kind of jerk and her pulses began to race. Half sitting as he was, she didn't have to look up at him, their eyes were almost level. There was no mistaking the message in his; that, or the way he slowly drew her towards him.

'Don't!' Leigh said sharply.

He looked amused and began to play with her fingers, twisting the ring her parents had given her for a twenty-first birthday present, and then going round to gently circle her palm. Leigh felt a surge of awareness run through her and tried to snatch her hand away. But he held it firmly.

'Will you please let go of me?'

'Why? You know you like it.'

'No.' But there was no conviction in her voice and he deliberately pulled her against him so that she was standing between his legs. Where the inside of his thighs touched her, she could feel the heat and hardness of his body against her own. He ran his hand through her hair, luxuriating in its rich softness. His thumb traced the line of her neck, her chin, and came to her mouth. A tremor of desire shook her, so strong that he felt it. His eyes darkened and putting his hands on her shoulders, he began to draw her towards him.

Leigh's eyes were drawn to his, held there, so that she felt like an animal, mesmerised by a danger that was too fascinating to run away from. A small sound of protest rose in her throat, but he merely smiled rather crookedly and placed his mouth on hers. His kiss was different this time, not hard and passionate, but soft and teasing, playing with her lips, biting softly. He gave so much but not enough, rousing a raw longing in her, making her want to push herself against him, feel the lean hardness of his body against the length of hers. She wanted him to exert his strength, dominate her with the power of his arms, impose his will with the passion of his mouth. Her lips moved under his, she said his name on a note almost of pleading. He laughed softly and Leigh jerked her head away.

She glared at him, her breathing unsteady and said on a sob, 'God, how I hate you, Bryce Allerton!'

His hands went to the buttons of her jacket, undid them and slid inside.

'You don't hate me—just the power that I have to make you feel like this.'

She could feel his hands exploring her breasts, hard and yet at the same time caressing. Her body arched, pushing against his hands. Then her arms went round his neck and she kissed him hungrily.

When she lifted her head she was trembling, her breath panting and unsteady. Bryce's right hand was still on her breast and his left he had put low down on her hips, pressing her close to him. Lifting a trembling hand to push the hair off her face, Leigh stared at him for a long moment, then stepped backwards and looked away, her face pale. This time he made no attempt to stop her, just sat and watched as she strove to recover some sort of composure. She looked round for the velvet ribbon for her hair and he silently picked it up and handed it to her. When she had fixed it over her hair she picked up her bag and put the weekend's schedule into it with hands that were still shaking. She couldn't speak to him, couldn't look at him, didn't trust herself not to go back into his arms. But when she turned towards the door he came up behind her and stopped her.

'Are you ready?'

'Ready?' She turned to look at him uncertainly.

'I'm going to take you out to dinner, and tonight we're definitely going back to my flat. We should have done last week. Tonight I'm not going to take no for an answer.' He smiled lazily down at her, arrogantly triumphant and sure that she was only too willing to do what he wanted.

Leigh looked past him at the office and suddenly remembered what Don Chapman had told her about Bryce's affair with the other pilot's wife, of the row that had taken place about it in this very room. Had the two of them made love here? she wondered. She felt cheapened by it, realising that she was just another conquest, to be taken and discarded when he grew tired of her. She had been supremely stupid and weak-willed to have let things go this far. But maybe it wasn't too late.

Turning to him, she said coldly, 'Well, I'm afraid you'll have to. I have no intention of going out with you tonight or any other night.'

She had the satisfaction of seeing him completely taken aback. Shock showed in his eyes before they hardened into a frown. 'You should know by now that I'm not the type you can play hot and cold with,' he informed her brusquely. 'And don't pretend that you don't want to go to bed with me— you made your needs more than plain just now.'

Leigh tried to regulate her breathing, tried to control the emotions his nearness was still arousing in her. She took a couple of determined steps away from him and said as levelly as she could, 'All right,

I'll admit that you turn me on . . .'

Bryce laughed harshly, 'Oh, I do a hell of a lot more than just turn you on!'

Her face reddening, Leigh went on doggedly as if he hadn't spoken, 'But I know even better now the type of man you are, and there's no way that I'm going to be just another name on your list, just another body to be used and discarded when you grow tired of it.'

His brows drew into a deeper frown and his voice was rough as he demanded, 'Just what have you heard about me?'

'Enough to know that I don't want to get involved with you.' She laughed mirthlessly. 'You know your trouble, Bryce? You're just too masculine and attractive for your own good. You can get any woman you want so easily that you've learnt to despise them, so you just treat them like dirt. But I . . .'

Bryce strode over to her and put an angry hand on her arm. 'Who's been talking to you? Tell me!'

'Does it matter?' she replied coldly.

For a moment longer he glared down at her angrily, then let go her arm and turned abruptly away as he said shortly, 'No, I don't suppose it does, if you're willing to believe any kind of gossip about me. If you let what you hear rule your own feelings and instincts.'

Puzzlement and uncertainty showed in Leigh's eyes when he said that, but then they cleared as she realised that that was the effect he had intended his words to have. She must remember that he was an old hand at this game, that he'd probably played this scene with other women in the past. And he knew how to handle it far better than she did, knew how to play on a woman's feelings until he had overcome all her scruples and had her eating out of his hand again. He turned to face her and she thought detachedly that he was a very good actor, one could almost believe that dark, rather fed-up look in his eyes if one didn't know exactly what he was trying to do.

Moving to the door, Leigh said coolly, 'If you'll excuse me, I'll be going. My date is waiting for me.' She needn't have added that last remark and felt rather annoyed with herself for having done so unnecessarily, but it had been a much-needed stab at his overflated ego.

'Another date?' Bryce commented, his voice dry. 'You must be getting quite serious. I take it it's the same man that you went out with on Wednesday?'

So he was taking note of who she went out with, was he? Oddly the idea pleased her. 'No, as a matter of fact it isn't,' she informed him shortly.

Bryce's eyebrows rose sardonically. 'A different man! And you've only been here two weeks. Obviously when it comes to fast workers, I'm not even in your league,' he observed snidely.

Leigh could have hit him. She even got as far as turning angrily to face him, but in time recognised the basic resentment in his tone. So he was jealous, was he? Good. Maybe it might teach him something, although she strongly suspected that this would be the first and last time he would ever feel the emotion. So instead she gave him a cool, provocative smile that brought a flare of anger to his grey eyes, then walked out of the door.

Bryce locked the door of his office, then followed

her down the stairs, the keys to lock the building for the night jangling in his hand. Leigh went to turn to the crew room to find Mike, but then caught sight of him through the glass doors, waiting for her in the reception area.

Bryce immediately guessed the situation and laughed derisively. 'So you've hooked Mike on your line, have you? That was to be expected. He's no good for you, Leigh.'

She turned to him exasperatedly. 'Will you please mind your own business?'

'It is my business when my employees start getting emotionally involved.'

'Oh, for God's sake, I'm only going out for a drink with him! And anyway, if it was all right for me to go out with you, then it's certainly all right for me to go out with Mike!'

'It isn't the same thing at all,' Bryce snapped back. 'I suppose it was Mike who poisoned your mind against me? And you of course believed him,' he added disgustedly.

'No,' Leigh retorted coldly, 'as a matter of fact it wasn't. Mike I might not have believed so readily, but Don Chapman I certainly did!'

She turned quickly away then, sickened by the whole thing, pushed open the door and walked up to Mike, giving him a brilliant smile and slipping her arm into his. 'Sorry to keep you waiting so long. Let's go, shall we?'

Mike perked up immediately, surprised and pleased by her greeting. He took her out to his sports car, leaving Bryce to lock up after them. As they drove away Leigh glanced back and saw Bryce watching them, a set, brooding look on his face.

She spent most of the evening regretting the warm way that she'd started it and trying to keep Mike at arm's length. That had been a mistake, as had not taking her own car, because now she was dependent on him to take her back to the airport to collect the Mini. That she had, definitely, been wrong in accepting Mike's invitation, Leigh discovered almost straight away. She had expected him to take her to a local pub, but instead he drove into Shepton Ferrers, to the huge new leisure complex where there was a big dance hall with a restaurant and several bars. They had a drink in one of these, but then he insisted on them having a meal in the restaurant and seemed to take it for granted that they would then go on to the disco. His presumption annoyed her; not only had she been looking forward to an evening at the cottage, but she was still wearing her working clothes; if she was going to a dance she liked to go home and bathe and change first. But perhaps Mike had realised that she would have said no if he'd suggested it.

Leigh hid her annoyance as best she could; after all, she did owe Mike for coming to her rescue this morning, and she tried to enjoy herself, but Mike's manner was a little too proprietorial for her to relax and be comfortable. He kept putting his arm round her waist whenever he led her back to her seat, or stood too close to her in between the records. Also, he kept asking her questions about herself, wanting to know about her past boyfriends and that kind of thing.

To change the subject Leigh asked him, 'Have you worked for Bryce for long?'

'A couple of years. It's just a stopgap until I can get on to a bigger airline.'

A long stopgap, Leigh thought privately, and if the economic climate stayed as it was he'd probably find himself at Allerton's for keeps—and lucky to be there, too.

'Bryce kept you a long time this afternoon,' Mike observed. 'He hadn't found out about the mix-up over the notes, had he?'

'Oh, no, nothing like that. He was just giving me the work schedule for the weekend.'

'He took long enough about it,' Mike paused, inviting her to give him a further explanation, but when she didn't speak, added rather lamely, 'Well, as long as he doesn't know.'

Leigh wasn't really listening, a thought had occurred to her and she said quickly, 'Mike, is there anything between Bryce and Carol?'

'Not that I know of, although there could be, of course. I think Carol probably fancies Bryce; I've seen her smiling at him and fluttering her eyelashes a few times, but I haven't seen him reciprocate. Why do you ask?'

'It's just that it was Carol who handed me the wrong notes this morning. She knows Bryce doesn't want me here and I think she's trying to get me fired.'

'It might not have been deliberate,' Mike pointed out. 'She might have picked the wrong ones up accidentally.'

'No, I'm sure she knew what she was doing. You see, she got me into trouble once before.' Briefly she explained about the log books.

'It looks as if you're right,' Mike admitted. 'But

why should she want to get rid of you? Unless she thinks that Bryce is interested in you, of course. Is he?' he asked, his eyes searching her face.

Leigh realised that she'd trapped herself, that she couldn't possibly tell Mike that Carol might have seen Bryce kissing her. 'Of course not,' she answered, over-emphatically. 'Carol probably just doesn't want any other girl around the place. After all, she's been the only woman here for some time, hasn't she?'

'Yes. But I think you're wrong. I've never heard of Bryce mixing business with pleasure.'

Leigh's eyes widened in surprised disbelief. 'Don't you call having an affair with that other pilot's wife mixing business with pleasure? Surely if he'd had any scruples Bryce would have refrained from making love to the woman behind his own pilot's back!' she finished disgustedly.

Mike was looking at her rather oddly. 'You—er—know about that?' he said slowly.

'Yes, Don told me.'

'Don did?' He sounded totally surprised.

'Yes.' She looked at him uncertainly. 'It is true, isn't it?

'What?' He hesitated a moment, then nodded and said, 'Oh, yes, it's true all right. I was just surprised at Don's telling you. What did he say exactly?'

Leigh repeated the little information the older pilot had given her and Mike grinned rather maliciously. 'Don didn't tell you the half of it. Bryce used to send the husband off on trips abroad so that he had the field clear to spend the night with the wife. And he used to boast about it in front of the pilot too,' he went on; then, seeing Leigh's look of horror, he added quickly, 'Oh, not directly, of course. He'd just make remarks about adultery in general and frustrated women, that kind of thing. It didn't mean anything to the husband at the time, but gave Bryce an extra kick, if you see what I mean?'

'Yes, I think I do,' Leigh agreed hollowly, fiercely glad now that she had rejected Bryce, and only wishing that he wasn't so damnably attractive and had this devastating effect on her whenever she was near him.

'You'll keep what I've told you under your hat, won't you?' Mike asked her. 'It's a taboo subject in the crew room. Better not mention it to Don again either—he was a friend of the pilot.'

She spent the rest of the evening keeping Mike at arm's length and eventually managed to get home at a cost of just a couple of kisses. Unfortunately Mike just didn't turn her on, although she had a terrible job trying to convince him of that. In a minor way he was as much of an egotist as Bryce was, but Mike would never have the same success, despite the glamour of his job, because he just didn't possess Bryce's magnetism and dominant male sexuality. He just wasn't in the same league.

Saturday and Sunday's flights passed by perfectly ordinarily and satisfactorily. Leigh enjoyed the trip to France and took the opportunity to do some shopping in a market there while she was waiting for the film crew, who, as Bryce had predicted, took a lot longer than they had said. And on Sunday the weather was bright and sunny for

the trip across to Bembridge Airport, on the Isle of
Wight. Her four passengers—two married
couples—were all in a good, holiday kind of mood,
laughing and joking, and they invited her to come
with them to look over the boats they were thinking
of purchasing. As she had nothing else to do Leigh
went with them and was amazed at the size and
sheer luxury of the vessels, and how businesslike
her passengers became when it got down to the
nitty-gritty of bargaining. They left about six and
flew back over the Solent, the sea reflecting like
faceted diamonds in the sunlight. Leigh looked at
the clear sky and hoped it would stay that way,
because tomorrow was her day off and she was to
fly the beloved Tiger Moth again for the first time
that year.

Getting up very early the next morning, Leigh
drove across country, heading for Hertfordshire. It
was a delightful spring day, sunny and with hardly
a breath of wind; a perfect flying day. Her spirits
rose as she drove, determinedly putting all thoughts
of Bryce behind her. The details that Mike had
given her had completed her disillusionment.
Instinct had played her false; Bryce just wasn't the
man she had hoped, and now she was going to
give her whole attention to flying. Flying didn't lift
you up to let you down again with a thud, it was
always fulfilling, consistently exciting. You could
do worse than have a love affair with the sky.
Much worse, she told herself ironically.

She fixed her thoughts on the Tiger Moth, an
old biplane that she owned in conjunction with
three other pilots. They had formed a syndicate
two years ago to buy the plane from the estate of

an old man who had owned it since it was made, but who had been too old and frail to fly it for a great many years, so that the Tiger had just stood in an old barn where it had steadily deteriorated because the old man couldn't afford to maintain it but couldn't bear to part with it. When he died it had at last been put up for sale and the four of them, all South-East Air pilots, had bought it and spent all their spare time lovingly restoring it to its original perfection. Now they kept it under moth-balls during the winter and helped to pay for its heavy maintenance costs by taking it to air shows during the summer months and putting on displays of aerobatics. And, today being a national holiday, there was to be an air show at a big country man-sion in Hertfordshire that was open to the public and had given its grounds over to an adventure park, steam railway, garden centre, miniature zoo—you name it, they had it.

The planes were to take off from a nearby small private airfield, do their act over the crowds of people who were assembling in the grounds of the mansion and then fly back to the airfield. One of her partners, Adam Hurst, was flying the Tiger Moth up from the airfield in Norfolk where they hired a hangar to house it, and they were each to give a flying demonstration, one in the morning and a second in the afternoon. Their other two partners were unable to come today, although usually they managed to all four get together whenever they could.

Today Adam had brought his new wife, Elaine, with him in the passenger seat, warmly wrapped up in a fur coat against the cold of the upper air,

as there was no cosy cockpit in the Tiger Moth, it
was completely open to the air. The Tiger was
painted scarlet and shone with the tender, loving
care that its owners lavished on it. As Adam's wife
remarked, it was a case of 'Love me—love my
plane,' and if she wanted to see anything of her
husband during the weekends then she had to go
along to help paint or polish, or to flying displays.

They had already arrived when Leigh drove up
and Adam was busy checking their place on the
programme with the organisers.

They were to put on the first display at noon
and the next at three. Tossing a coin to decide who
should go first, Adam won, which pleased his wife.
'Good, now you can take me up to the air show so
that I can take a look round the stately home.'

Adam laughed. 'All right, if that's what you
want. Mind if we borrow your Mini, Leigh?'

'No, of course not.'

They had a very enjoyable time wandering round
the airfield, looking at other planes and talking to
their pilots, many of whom they knew from other
air shows during the last two years. Their display
was to follow that of three helicopters who did
formation flying. Adam got the thumbs-up signal
from the organiser when the helicopters were just
about finished and took off, flying high so that he
would be above the helicopters on their way back.
The two girls fell silent as they waited for him to
return; aerobatics in itself wasn't dangerous if it
was carried out properly, but with any stunt flying
there was always an element of risk where some
lack of concentration for a fraction of a second
could bring disaster. Over in the distance they saw

intertwining spirals of red and blue smoke drifting up into the air and knew that Adam had completed his performance. It had only taken about ten minutes, but Leigh could guarantee that the crowds had been holding their breath for most of that time.

The three of them had a picnic lunch sitting on a rug beside the plane. Leigh had brought most of the stuff with her that she had bought in the French market and Elaine Hurst had also brought some food, so they had quite a feast. Around them nearly all the other pilots were doing the same thing, but the remarkable difference between these and any other picnics was that hardly anyone was drinking alcohol, all the fliers were washing down their meals with soft drinks.

After lunch Adam helped Leigh to get the Tiger Moth ready for the next display, then he took Elaine off in the Mini. Leigh spent a little more time chatting, but at two-thirty climbed into the Tiger and went through the act from first to last in her mind, mentally preparing herself for the extreme concentration she would need during the performance. Ten minutes before she was due to take off she put on the extra layers of clothing she was going to need to keep her warm in the air: an extra pair of padded trousers, thick sweater with a fur-lined flying jacket over it, scarf, gloves and a cloth flying-helmet. With all that lot on, there wasn't a great deal of room in the cockpit, which was just as well; it wasn't very comfortable if you slid around in your seat while doing aerobatics. Leigh fastened the ordinary safety straps and then the second, precautionary harness that they'd added just in case. She started the engine and let it run for a few minutes, getting used to its noisy buzz that excluded all other sounds, breathing in the oil, glue and aircraft-dope smells that you always got with old fabric planes.

Her signal to start was given and Leigh opened the throttle to taxi across the uneven grass on to the runway. She took off into the sun and climbed high and straight before turning towards the show-ground. A thousand feet below her she saw the three black and yellow helicopters going by in a perfect V formation, looking like giant dragonflies. When the show ground came in sight she climbed higher, then reduced speed to fifty knots, holding up the nose until the plane stalled and the right wing flipped over. Then the Tiger began to spin fast as it dived downwards standing on its nose, getting ever closer to the ground, the shadows thrown by the wing struts passing over her and coming full circle again, the noise of the air changing from a sigh to a rushing scream. When the crowds below were craning upwards, holding their concerted breath, certain that she would dive straight into the ground, Leigh kicked hard on the left rudder bar and then pulled back for the final loop that put her on to level flight skimming above the ground.

She went on with the display of low-level aerobatics, flying from side to side across the ground in front of the crowd, doing loops and rolls-off-the-top, flying upside down, the blood thundering in her ears. Twisting and tumbling through the air, pushing the Tiger to its limits, but careful not to get into a slow roll which would make the engine snarl and stall. Concentrating for every second of the time, her nerves cool as ice. As the final part of the act, she came in low from the west, clicking on a switch which released the smoke canisters that were attached to each end of the lower wings. The smoke billowed out behind her in two long trails, one red, the other blue, as she rolled and began to do spiralling turns horizontally across the showground, keeping the plane always at the same height, just high enough off the ground for the wings to clear it every time she turned, but leaving no margin at all for mistakes. One slip or error of judgement and the plane would have been scattered in pieces and Leigh along with it.

At the other end of the ground, she climbed quickly to avoid the marquees and tents and dipped her wings in a last salute to the crowds before heading back to the airfield. Leigh hoped that they were clapping, that they had enjoyed her performance; she had certainly given of her best, but she had no way of knowing. It was impossible to hear any ground noises up here; it was like performing on a stage to an audience of mutes. After landing, Leigh taxied over to their parking place, waited several minutes for the engine to cool down and then switched if off, but had to wait for a few minutes longer until the buzz of the engine finally receded from her ears. She climbed stiffly out of the cockpit, feeling suddenly tired now that the adrenalin pumped into her bloodstream by the stunt flying had slowed down, and began to divest herself of all the extra clothing, putting it back into the cockpit ready for Adam to wear when he took the Tiger home.

'Just what the hell do you think you're playing at?'

The furiously angry voice behind her made Leigh jerk round in startled surprise. A car had driven up across the grass, its engine almost non-existent beneath the noise of the helicopters which had re-fuelled and were heading back to their home base. The car had come to a halt about ten yards away. It was a Jaguar, and Bryce had climbed out of it and was striding across the grass towards her, his face contorted by rage.

Leigh gaped at him, stunned to see him there at all, her mind not yet taking it in.

'You could have been killed doing that kind of crazy stunt flying!' Bryce thundered as he came up to her, angrier than she had ever seen him before, and that was saying something.

Leigh blinked and found her voice. 'What are you doing here?'

'Never mind what I'm doing here,' he snarled. 'Just who the hell said you could go round throwing a plane about in the air like that?'

'I don't understand what you mean. I didn't have to ask anyone if I could,' she answered in some bewilderment.

'Well, I'm *telling* you that this is the last time. In future you keep away from stunt flying, d'you hear me?'

Leigh heard him all right; and she was un-comfortably aware that everyone within ten yards of them had also heard. Her own temper began to rise and she said shortly, 'And just what has it got to do with you what I do in my own time?'

'Everything, so long as you're working for me.

Just how do you think my charter customers and passengers are going to feel when they know that one of my pilots indulges in aerobatics for a hobby?'

'Oh, for heaven's sake,' Leigh answered exasperatedly. 'Lots of airline pilots do stunt or formation flying in their spare time. And anyway, how could any of your customers ever know?'

'How could they not know when the fact that "Leigh Bishop, the courageous girl flyer, who is currently working for Allerton's Air Charters" was announced to the whole crowd over the public address system?' he demanded, his voice heavy with sarcasm as he repeated the words. 'You know as well as I do how quickly news gets around in this industry.'

Surprised, Leigh said, 'But how could the organisers know that? I didn't tell them.'

'Don't put on that innocent act with me! You know darn well that I wouldn't . . .'

'Is something the matter, Leigh?'

Adam's voice interrupted them and Leigh turned towards him gratefully. She was about to explain, but Bryce broke in harshly. 'Who the hell are you?'

It was the wrong thing to say to Adam. He was nowhere near as big as Bryce, but he didn't take that kind of thing from anybody. His jaw jutted forward and he squared his shoulders threateningly.

'He's with me,' Leigh broke in hastily. 'He's my . . .'

'Oh, just another one of your many lovers, is

he?' Bryce put in before she could finish, his tone insulting.

'I don't know who you damn well think you are,' Adam said hotly, 'but you'll take that back, right now!'

His hands closed into fists and he brought his right arm back to punch Bryce on the nose. Leigh saw Bryce squaring up to do the same thing and hurriedly grabbed Bryce's arm, the horror of the two men having a public brawl frightening the life out of her. Bryce tried to shake her off, but she clung on, and then Elaine laughed and calmly walked between the two men.

She stood in front of her husband and turned to Bryce with a smile. 'I certainly hope he isn't Leigh's lover, because he happens to be my husband—and a very new husband at that!'

Bryce stared down at her for a moment, bewildered by her sudden appearance between them. As her words got through, Leigh felt some of the tension go out of his arm, but she still hung on, afraid that he was still angry enough to take a punch at Adam over Elaine's head.

'Now, what's this all about?' the other girl was asking. She turned to look at Adam and pushed him gently a little farther away. 'Do you two realise what an exhibition you're making of yourselves— or how many people are standing around gaping at you?' she added loud enough for the avidly interested onlookers to overhear.

The spectators hurriedly turned away and pretended they hadn't been watching and listening at all; while Bryce and Adam looked round rather shamefacedly, realising just how close they'd come to fighting like a couple of schoolboys. Leigh gave a sigh of relief and let go of Bryce's arm. He turned his head to look at her, a strange, puzzled kind of frown between his eyes. He started to say something, but Adam spoke to her first.

'Just who is he, anyway?'

'He's my boss. His name is Bryce Allerton. And he's mad at me because it was announced over the P.A. system that I'm working for him.' She looked at Bryce and repeated, with no expectation of being believed, 'But I honestly didn't tell them.'

'No. I did,' Adam stated baldly. 'What's wrong with that?'

Leigh waited for Bryce to say exactly what he thought was wrong with it, but he still had that puzzled, abstracted look and stayed strangely silent, so Leigh said for him, 'Bryce thinks it will put his customers off flying with his company.'

'Rubbish,' Adam retorted. 'It only proves what an extremely good pilot you are. You're damn lucky to have her on your payroll,' he added, addressing Bryce directly.

Leigh quaked inwardly. It was wonderful of Adam to stick up for her like this, but couldn't he see that it would only make Bryce angry again and bring his wrath down on her head?

She waited for the storm to break and then stared at him in stunned incredulity as he merely said, 'So everyone keeps telling me. Maybe it's about time I started listening.'

His eyes came down to meet Leigh's as he spoke, holding them as she looked up at him wonderingly. Elaine and Adam watched them, then glanced at each other and exchanged a knowing smile.

'Well,' Elaine said brightly, 'now that we've got that sorted out, why don't we all have a drink of something? There's still quite a lot left in the picnic hamper. My name's Elaine, by the way,' she added, thrusting out a hand to Bryce.

He shook it and gave her a lazy smile, apparently quite recovered from his strange abstraction of a moment ago. 'Thank you, a drink would be most welcome.'

So instead of ending up as a nasty incident, they found themselves sitting on the grass drinking coffee and eating sandwiches. Thanks to Elaine. Leigh sat next to her and gave her a speaking look of gratitude. It wasn't long before the two men were deep into a conversation about the relative merits of various aircraft, their differences of a few minutes before gone and forgotten. Leigh took advantage of this to lean over to Elaine and say feelingly, 'Thanks. If it hadn't been for you I'm sure they would have started fighting.'

Elaine grinned. 'Can you imagine what we looked like? Those two idiots yelling at each other and us trying to pull them apart!'

The mental picture was so funny that they both began to giggle and ended up laughing helplessly. This caught the attention of the two men, who had little doubt that they were the object of all the hilarity. Adam looked at Bryce and summed up their joint masculine attitude, by saying loftily, 'Women!' and resuming the conversation where they had left off.

When they'd recovered from their laughter, Leigh interrupted and said to Bryce, 'Just what *are* you doing here, anyway?'

'I brought along some advertising material for Allerton's to put up in one of the display tents. You get all sorts of people bringing their kids here for a day out, and you never know who might come along and realise that an air charter is just the thing he needs for his business.' He looked at Adam and nodded towards the Tiger. 'Is it your plane?'

'No, Leigh and I are co-owners with two others. We share the costs equally between us and take it in turns to fly it at this sort of thing, or at vintage aircraft rallies.'

'Must be expensive,' Bryce commented.

Adam grinned. 'It helps to keep us poor, admittedly. But we're used to that, aren't we, love?' He looked at his wife and the grin changed to a smile that was so full of love that Leigh had to look hastily away, feeling that she was intruding on something very private. At the same time she felt her own heart tear with envy and longing.

She felt a hand touch her shoulder and looked up to find Bryce standing over her, cutting out the sun. 'Why don't you show me over your plane?'

He held out his hand to her and Leigh slowly gave him hers and let him pull her to her feet. She avoided his eyes and instead looked down at the others, but they had moved closer together and were still wrapped up in each other. Bryce hadn't let go of her hand and his grip tightened. She tried to draw away, but he held on and so she had to slowly, reluctantly meet his eyes. He was looking at her almost as if seeing her for the first time and wanted to memorise her features, his grey eyes fixed on her intently. Leigh's heart gave a crazy kind of leap and she turned hastily away, pulling

her hand free. She walked over to the plane and
began to talk quickly—much too quickly—to try
and hide her feelings. 'We bought the plane about
two years ago from a man who'd had it from new.'
She gabbled on, pointing out all the interesting
features she could think of, telling him its entire
history.

Bryce followed her as they walked round the
plane, just letting her talk, listening and watching
her. At length Leigh couldn't think of anything else
to say and turned to him rather lamely. 'Well, I
guess that's about it.'

'Thank you,' said Bryce on a note of gentle
amusement. 'It was very comprehensive.'

Leigh coloured a little and said awkwardly,
'Perhaps you'd like to sit in the cockpit?'

'I'd like that very much.' He climbed in the front
seat and put his hand on the stick, looking over
the control panel. 'It's a long time since I've been
up in one of these,' he remarked reminiscently.

'Have you ever flown one?'

He shook his head regretfully. 'No, but I'd love
to try.' He glanced down to where she stood beside
the plane. 'How about taking me up?'

Leigh gazed at him for a minute, then answered
stiltedly, 'You're welcome to a ride, of course.'
Turning, she raised her voice and said, 'Hey,
Adam, you've got a passenger! Bryce wants a joy-
ride.'

Adam goodnaturedly got to his feet and ambled
over. 'Sure. But don't you want to take him up?'

'I've only just got warm again. And besides,
you'll be able to tell him all the technical bits that
I'm no good at.'

'Okay, we'd better get kitted up.'

Leigh went and sat by Elaine, carefully avoiding looking directly at Bryce, although she knew he was watching her. The men put on all the extra clothing and climbed into the cockpit, Bryce in the front seat. He lifted a hand to Leigh and said compellingly, 'See you later.' They took off as soon as the runway was clear, heading in the opposite direction to the air show, which was just about coming to an end.

The two girls watched it climb and become a small red dot in the blueness of the sky. 'How long have you been working for Bryce, Leigh?' Elaine asked.

'Not long, only about two weeks.'

'How do you get on with him?'

Leigh laughed rather harshly. 'We've hardly stopped rowing with one another since the first time we met! He thought I was a man, you see, and was rather put out when I turned out to be a girl.'

'Well, you certainly seem to strike sparks off one another,' Elaine commented. She gave Leigh a sidelong glance. 'He's very attractive. Do you fancy him?'

Leigh didn't answer for a minute, then she said slowly, 'Fancying him would be a very stupid and self-destructive thing to do. He's a stud. He even goes with married women.' Abruptly she got to her feet. 'It's getting late and I've a long drive ahead of me. Say goodbye to Adam for me, will you? Tell him I'll be in touch before the next air show.'

Elaine didn't try to stop her and soon Leigh was making her way back through the country lanes towards home. She knew that those last words from Bryce had been an explicit order to wait for him, but she hadn't wanted to see him again. Just as she hadn't wanted to carry on that conversation with Elaine, because she didn't want to have to admit that she had just discovered that she was in love with a man whose morals she despised.

CHAPTER SIX

THE next day was a hectic one at Allerton's; not only did they have a lost day to make up, but Mike was also starting to fly the car company's executives in the new Navajo. Leigh did the vegetable run and wished heartily that the British onions would hurry up and come into season so that they didn't have to import French ones any more. These vegetables, she had found out, were for really top class hotels who insisted on the very freshest foods for their patrons. When she got back, Carol told her there was another job for her and she was given a short trip over to East Midlands Airport to collect a metal mould which a plastics firm needed in a great hurry.

Leigh had been hoping that she wouldn't run into Bryce that day, but he was on the tarmac talking to Vic when she landed for the second time. He fell into step beside her as she walked over to the crew room.

'I wanted to see you to give you this.'

He handed her an envelope and Leigh took it slowly. 'What is it?'

'It's your pay cheque.'

But she hadn't been there for a month yet. She looked fixedly down at the envelope as if it could tell her what she wanted to know. She was trying to form the words to ask him when Bryce spoke again.

131

'I've got a new pilot starting later on this week, by the way. He's an ex-Dan Air man.'

Leigh came to a stop and turned to face him. 'Are you telling me that I'm fired?'

His left eyebrow rose. 'Why should you think that?'

'You pay me my money a week before it's due, and then tell me you're taking on a new pilot. What am I supposed to think, for heaven's sake?'

'Everyone gets paid on the first of the month, so yours has been worked out accordingly. It would be too inconvenient to pay each person monthly on the day he started. And as for the new pilot, I'm taking him on because Mike will probably be flying more or less full-time for the car company. I'm not about to ask you to leave, Leigh,' he added, his voice contained a more gentle note than she had ever imagined it could hold.

'Oh, I see,' she answered inadequately. Then, rather waspishly, 'I hope you checked that he really is a *he*, this time.'

Bryce laughed. 'Most definitely. I insisted he send me a photograph with his application. And then, not many girls are called Robert.'

'Not unless they're really Roberta and they like wearing butch clothes and hairstyle,' Leigh quipped.

He laughed again, his grey eyes alight with it. 'Speaking from your own experience, how would you advise her to handle the situation?'

Steadily she answered, 'I'd tell her to tear up her contract and get the hell out before she made the mistake of starting.'

His face changed at once, the amusement fleeing

from his eyes as they became serious, even
troubled. 'Why didn't you wait for me yesterday?'

'There wasn't any point,' she told him, stony-
faced.

His voice suddenly became forceful and he put a
hand on her arm to emphasise it. 'Leigh, you've
got absolutely the wrong idea about me. I don't
know what Don Chapman told you, and as he's
on holiday in America I can't get him to put it
right. But I'm asking you to trust me and believe
me. Will you, Leigh? Will you trust me?'

Bewildered by his urgency, Leigh looked up at
him uncertainly. It would be so easy to believe him,
and she wanted to—so very much. But there was
so much against him and he had given no explanation, or even attempted to make one.

'No,' she answered shortly. 'Why should I?'

Bryce flinched back as if she'd hit him. 'No
reason,' he said coldly. 'No reason at all,' and
stepped back so that she could go into the crew
room, then turned on his heel and went back to
the hangar.

The early payment was a godsend. Leigh took
the opportunity of a wait between flights the next
day to slip into Shepton Ferrers to bank the cheque
and draw out some cash. Then she had a mini-
shopping spree, buying a new blouse and pair of
denim jeans, as well as stocking up in the food
line, including some of the goodies that she'd had
to forgo during the last weeks, like ground coffee
and steak. That evening she had a pleasant time
putting away her purchases, washing her hair with
a new luxury shampoo, and making herself a meal
of stuffed avocado, followed by steak and a salad.

It ought to have been a perfect meal and a perfect evening, but it wasn't. Oh, the steak was beautifully cooked, her hair looked good, and it was lovely to have the flowers that she'd bought to brighten up the cottage. But her mind kept going back to Bryce. She had been right to reject him, there could be no doubt about that, but she felt so empty and alone. Her sexual appetities were as normal as anyone else's and she had been turned on by men before, but she'd never felt this need, this longing for a man to hold her, to touch and be touched, this dreadful urgency in her body for love and fulfilment. She sat on the settee and looked at the empty grate in which she'd put a large copper vase full of flowers, and tears of frustration and unhappiness ran down her cheeks.

Luckily the next day was sunny, so she had an excuse to wear dark glasses and hide the puffiness that still showed round her eyes. On seeing her face in the mirror this morning she had cursed herself for a stupid, lovesick fool. The man was no good to her or to any other woman, so why cry for something she was well rid of? And what good did crying do anyway? It was just a despicable female weakness, made use of by some women as a weapon when they wanted to get round some poor fool of a man.

Leigh managed to avoid Bryce as much as possible, getting into the habit of taking the car to the nearest piece of parkland whenever she had a longish wait between runs, and spending the time sitting on a bench there instead of in the crew room. It wasn't so easy, though, to avoid Mike, because he made a point of looking up her schedule and trying to be on hand whenever she was due to come in or out. He persistently asked for another date, and twice even called her over the radio when she was flying, which she didn't go much on. At first she refused him as politely as she knew how, but in the end had to turn round and tell him she just wasn't interested. He thought far too much of himself to accept it gracefully, of course, and stalked off, deeply offended.

On Friday evening Leigh met the new pilot, who was in his mid-forties and glad to have found another job in flying. She worked on the Saturday morning but had the rest of the weekend free to work on the garden of the cottage, which had become a little neglected since its owner had been away, despite Don's efforts. It was a rewarding job and one which ordinarily Leigh would have enjoyed, but this time she didn't, and she wished she could have been working instead. Because gardening gave you too much time to think, and right now her thoughts were full of Bryce, of what might have been, and of what could be if she hadn't any pride. Often she would pause, with garden fork or hedge clippers in her hands, and gaze into space picturing what might have happened if she'd gone back to his flat with him as he'd wanted. Then her body would surge with the heat of frustrated yearning until she came rudely back to reality, and she would try and pull herself together and go on with her task, but always the thoughts and emotions came flooding back to torture her again.

When she flew in one afternoon during the following week, Leigh found a message waiting for her on the crew room notice board asking her to see

Bryce. Slowly she took down the piece of paper and read it over again, wondering what it portended. She put the interview off as long as possible, first writing up her logs and records, then going to the Ladies' to freshen up, but at last she couldn't put it off any longer and climbed the stairs to his office.

He was dictating letters to Carol. Leigh said with some relief, 'Oh, sorry, I'll come back later,' but he beckoned her into the room.

'This won't take more than a minute.'

He went on dictating while Leigh went over to the window and looked out on to the tarmac. There were four planes standing there at the moment in the smart turquoise and white livery of Allerton's Air Charters: the oldish plane they used only for freight, the small Arrow, an Aztec, and the beautiful new Navajo. And there were two more planes in the air. Not bad at all. In fact any air company that could expand instead of putting people off at the moment must be well managed. Not that she'd ever doubted it; she was quite sure that if anyone survived it would be Bryce. He was a born fighter—and a born winner. The thought made her shiver and she gripped the top of the radiator below the window.

'Okay, Carol, that's it. The first three letters I'd like to go off tonight, but you can leave the others until tomorrow morning.'

Leigh waited, not looking round, until she heard the door shut behind the other girl, then she braced herself and turned reluctantly to face him. Her first thought was that he looked different, rather tired and a little thinner in the face, and she felt immediate concern, but then realised that this was probably only a result of the kind of lifestyle he led. Perhaps he'd been having a lot of late nights—or a lot of early ones with his latest mistress, Leigh thought cynically.

Bryce studied her for a moment, noting the set look to her mouth, and said shortly, 'It's come to my notice that you and Mike made an unscheduled landing at Elstree Aerodrome a week or so ago. I'd like to know why.'

Well, Mike certainly hadn't wasted any time in getting his own back, Leigh thought with resigned bitterness; she supposed she ought to have expected something like this.

'I'm sure Mike must have explained why when he told you that we landed there,' she answered.

Bryce's dark brows flickered and he said, 'Suppose you give me your explanation.'

Leigh shrugged. 'It was my fault entirely. There was a mix-up over the collection and delivery notes. I was given his and he got mine, so we landed at Elstree because it was the nearest point where we could swop them over.'

'You said that you were given the wrong notes. Who gave them to you?'

'What does it matter? It was my responsibility to check them before I took off, and I didn't.'

'Why didn't you?'

She laughed mirthlessly, remembering that it was because she'd been so flustered by his kiss. 'I had something else on my mind at the time,' she replied tartly.

He let that go, but asked, 'Was it Carol who caused the mix-up?' Leigh lowered her head and

didn't answer. She was still standing with her back
to the window, the sun coming in to shine on to
her chestnut hair, creating a brilliant glowing
aureole around her head. After a moment Bryce
went on, 'If Carol has taken a dislike to you, you'll
have to handle it yourself, Leigh; I don't want to
have to get involved.'

'All right.' That was fair enough, she could
understand his reluctance to interfere in something
so petty and spiteful.

She expected him to heap coals of fire on her
head, not only for the mix-up but also for trying to
cover it up, but he said nothing more about it, and
Leigh thanked her stars for having got let off so
lightly. She moved to leave, but he said, 'Don't go
yet, there are a couple more things.' Picking up a
sheet of paper from his desk, he looked at it, then
up at her. 'You've been working here for a full
calendar month now; do you wish to go on to our
permanent staff?'

Leigh put her hands on the back of the chair
facing his desk and gripped it hard. 'Are you
saying that you're prepared to keep me on? After
all?'

Bryce put the paper down on the desk and
dropped his hands below the desk where she
couldn't see them. 'Yes, I'm willing to have you
stay on. I'll admit that you're a good pilot and you
do the job well. And you've fitted in here much
better than I ever expected you to.'

Leigh stared at him, lips parted in surprise, quite
unprepared for such a handsome admission that
he'd been wrong. Then her eyes met his and she
quickly looked away. 'Thank you,' she mumbled.

'Well, do you want to stay on?' he repeated after a moment.

Leigh looked down at her knuckles, showing white as they gripped the back of the chair. She ought to say no, to take the opportunity to get away and start a new life as far away from here as possible, to put Bryce behind her and try and forget him. She tried to say it, her mouth forming the word, but somehow it came out as 'Yes'.

'Very well, you can consider yourself on the permanent payroll. Now,' he sorted out another paper, 'I've had an offer of a rather unusual taxi run which will last all next week, Monday to Friday. It's from the actress Faye Winter. Have you heard of her?'

'Why, yes, she's in a play in the West End at the moment, isn't she? An Alan Ayckbourn comedy. It's been running for quite some time.'

'Almost a year,' Bryce agreed. 'And that's Faye Winter's difficulty. She has one more week to go in the play before her contract ends, but she also wants to do a television play starting on Monday. Normally there wouldn't be any problem as the theatre only does Saturday matinees, but this particular play is being filmed on location in Devon. So the only way she can do both is by flying down to Devon early every morning, and then fly back again in time for the evening performance at the theatre.' He sat back in his chair and looked at her. 'Would you be willing to take it on—bearing in mind that you'd have to be at Heathrow to pick her up at seven in the morning and you probably wouldn't get back here until about seven in the evening? It's a pretty long day, although you'll have plenty of time to rest while you're waiting in Devon.'

'I'd like to,' Leigh answered at once. 'Very much.'

'Good, that's settled. I'll phone Faye Winter straight away.' His glance flicked up to her again. 'Your home is in Devon, isn't it?'

'Yes, near Tavistock.'

'Then, if you can arrange it, you'll be able to visit your family.'

'Yes.' Coming round the chair, she sat down in it and asked rather tentatively, 'Is that why you gave me the job rather than one of the other pilots—so that I could visit my home?'

Bryce hesitated a moment, then shook his head rather ruefully. 'I'd love to be able to say it was, but unfortunately I didn't have any altruistic reason. As a matter of fact Faye Winter asked for you personally.'

'She did?' Leigh's eyes flew wide in surprise. 'But how could she? She doesn't even know me.'

'But she knows *of* you.' Bryce's lips twisted in irony. 'It seems that a fellow actor was the guest celebrity at the air show and saw your performance. And he told Faye Winter about you.'

Her brow creased into a frown, Leigh said, 'But I still don't see . . .'

'It's because she has so little time in between the T.V. film and the play that she'll have to change costumes during the flight,' Bryce explained. 'And she was afraid that taking off her clothes right there beside him might make any ordinary pilot lose his concentration, so she decided that a female pilot was just what she needed.'

'Oh.' Leigh looked at him, remembering how mad he'd been with her for taking part. 'Oh,' she said again, then, 'Well, you *did* say you never knew who might go there and find they need an air charter!'

And suddenly they were both laughing, Bryce ruefully and Leigh with nervous relief.

'It seems I'm being proved wrong in all sorts of ways recently,' he commented after a few moments. 'And one of them in the most basic way of all.'

His face and voice had grown serious again. She gave him a swift glance and found him watching her. Getting to her feet, she said, 'Is that everything?'

'For now. I'll let you know the exact times later.'

'Thank you.' She moved towards the door and Bryce stood up and followed her, opening it for her.

'Oh, by the way,' he remarked just as she went past him, 'have you and Mike had a quarrel?'

Leigh paused and looked up at him uneasily; he had a habit of keeping one punch to the last. 'Why should you think that?' she temporised.

'Because you seemed to think that it was Mike who'd told me about your landing at Elstree.'

'Wasn't it?'

'No, as a matter of fact it was the airfield manager at Elstree. He sent a routine promotion letter giving the registration numbers of your planes and saying that he was glad we'd been able to use his field, and hoping Allerton's would be able to make use of its facilities again in the future.'

'Have you spoken to Mike about it?'

'Not yet.'

'I see,' Leigh observed dryly, realising how neatly she'd fallen into his trap.

'But don't worry—I intend to. Mike knows the rules better than you do,' he added grimly.

'Look, I've already told you it was all my fault,' Leigh protested.

Bryce's hand gripped the edge of the door and his mouth thinned. 'Still sticking up for him? Maybe you haven't quarrelled after all.'

'No, I haven't had a row with him.' She saw the bleak look that came into Bryce's grey eyes and something made her add, 'I don't know him well enough to quarrel with him.' Then she turned and hurried away before she saw the swift, speculative look he gave her.

Piloting Faye Winter was a joy. Leigh picked her up at Heathrow at seven on Monday morning and found the actress all ready and waiting so that she had a very fast turn-around.

Settling herself into the front passenger seat, she turned to smile at Leigh and apologised for having got her up so early and for having to do such an arduous trip. She was an extremely charming woman and all her charm came though in that smile and in her warm, rich voice, so that Leigh was immediately captivated.

Leigh smiled back and said impulsively, 'Oh, that's all right, Miss Winter. You're a great improvement on French onions and fish!'

'I am?' the actress demanded in amazement. 'How come?' So Leigh explained about her usual Monday morning run, which made the other

woman laugh, and soon they were on first name
terms and discussing important matters like clothes
and make-up. This last because Faye Winter had
brought a professional make-up case with her,
rather like a wooden attache case, which opened
up to show a large mirror fixed into the lid and
lots of compartments for various items of make-up
built into the base.

'Try and fly as steadily as possible will you, darling?' she asked. 'There won't be time to make up
when I get there so I'll have to do it on the way.'

By the time they flew into Roborough Airport
near Plymouth, Faye Winter looked at least fifteen
years younger. Leigh guessed her age to be in the
early thirties, but now she looked almost like a
teenager, the tiny telltale lines of age magically dis-
appearing under the skilfully applied theatrical
make-up.

'I have to age from sixteen to nearly seventy, so
I have to look as young as I possibly can to start
with,' she explained.

'All in one play?' Leigh exclaimed.

'Oh, no. This is a thirteen-part serial. It's one of
those family sagas set in the nineteenth century.
We make about one episode a week if everything
goes okay.'

'But that's a terribly punishing schedule. How
can you possibly keep it up?'

'It's only for this week; I finish in the West End
play on Saturday and then I'll rent a house down
in Devon until the serial finishes so that I don't
have to commute.' Faye Winter smiled rather
grimly. 'I've spent too long "resting" in the past to
turn down a good offer now, even if it does mean

that I only get about four hours sleep every night for a week.'

When they landed she was whisked away in a large car to the location site a few miles down the coast, and Leigh was picked up by her mother in their modest family car to spend a happy and much-needed day with her parents and younger brother.

On the return journey, Faye Winter got into the back of the plane, where she took off her television make-up and changed into a slinky black evening dress which was her opening costume for the play. Then she hitched up her skirts and gave Leigh a leg-show as she climbed into the front seat, where she opened her make-up box again and put on a new face, this time looking more her own age but with each feature emphasised for the sake of the theatre audience. She didn't seem to mind being watched or talking while she worked, so for a while Leigh put the plane on auto-pilot and looked on in fascination at her adeptness, asking one or two questions and receiving several useful tips.

Afterwards they talked of other things and found they had several interests in common, but as Heathrow grew nearer Leigh had to stop talking and give all her attention to the approach. There were too many big speedbirds flying around these skies to relax your concentration for even a second.

As the week progressed the two girls became even more friendly, and somehow Leigh found herself telling Faye about her feelings for Bryce. It was on Thursday evening as they were flying back to London. Bryce had just got through to her over the radio and asked her if she wanted to do a charter up to Scotland on Sunday, which she'd accepted. Faye began to ask her about her work, but Leigh answered only abstractedly. It was the first time she had spoken to Bryce for almost a week and just the sound of his voice made her insides go wobbly.

Faye looked at her searchingly, asked one or two shrewd questions, and suddenly Leigh started telling her all about Bryce.

'You mean he actually said that you could only keep your job if you went to bed with him?'

'Well, no,' Leigh admitted, thinking back. 'He didn't actually *say* it, but he certainly implied it.'

'And yet you say he's keeping you on anyway?'

'Yes. It's strange.'

'Maybe you were mistaken.'

'But if I was, why didn't he deny it when I accused him?'

Faye shrugged and laughed. 'I don't know. Men can be funny creatures sometimes, especially when their pride comes into it.'

'Well, there can be no doubt that he's a womaniser,' Leigh told her flatly. 'He has quite a reputation.'

'But you can hardly expect a man of thirty-five to have lived like a monk all his life, can you?' Faye pointed out. 'He could hardly call himself a man if he did. And from the way you describe him he sounds terrifically good-looking and virile. A super-stud in fact, so no wonder women go for him.' She laughed again. 'In fact I wouldn't mind meeting him myself!'

Leigh smiled. 'Maybe I exaggerated a little.'

'Maybe you're biased. Are you very much in love with him, Leigh?' the older girl asked gently.

'Crazy about him,' she admitted in a flippant tone that couldn't hide the emotion underneath.

'So why don't you sleep with him? Maybe you'll find out that he cares about you too.'

'No.' Leigh slowly shook her head. 'It would hurt too much if he didn't care. And I don't believe that he does, even though he said ...' She broke off uncertainly.

'Though he said what?' Faye prompted.

'Well, once he said that I'd got the wrong idea about him and he asked me to trust him.'

'And you turned him down flat, I suppose,' Faye commented dryly.

'Yes, I suppose I did.'

'Leigh, you idiot! You could at least have given the guy a chance. What have you got to lose?'

Leigh was silent for a moment, her hands gripping the half-wheel of the control yoke, then she answered haltingly, 'Because I'm afraid. I'm afraid that it will be just another affair for him. If I gave myself to him I'd never be able to relax completely because in the back of my mind I'd always be wondering if that would be the last time, whether tomorrow he'd throw me over for someone else. I could never be completely happy with him, and once he did tire of me I should probably be bitter about it for the rest of my life.'

'Wow!' Faye sighed. 'You really have got it badly!'

'Yes,' Leigh agreed. 'And the strange thing is that if I didn't love him I could probably go to bed with him and have a marvellous time, and then

just walk away with no hard feelings. Ironic, isn't
it?'

'Not really. But it's not just sex you want, my
girl, it's love. And what makes you so sure that he
isn't in love with you anyway? He asked you to
trust him, didn't he?'

'That was just a line.'

'Maybe. Maybe not. When men get lonely, Leigh,
they turn to women for companionship, and the
longer they remain a bachelor the more women
they turn to in that time, so it's hardly surprising
that your Bryce has got something of a reputation.
But that doesn't mean he isn't going to fall madly
in love at some stage of his life. And maybe you're
it, if you see what I mean. And believe me, darling,
there's no man more faithful than a reformed
playboy. They make far better husbands than men
who haven't had time to sow their wild oats before
they marry, so go off the rails at about forty-five
because they suddenly realise that they've missed
out on life and if they don't hurry up it's going to
be too late.'

Faye stopped and laughed at herself. 'Lord, I
sound like one of those Agony Aunts, don't I? But
I mean it, Leigh. At least give him the chance to
show you how he feels. You don't have to commit
yourself by going to bed with him; just go out with
him a few times.'

'Somehow with Bryce I don't think just going
out together would be enough,' Leigh answered
dryly.

'It will if he loves you. Oh, not for long, perhaps,
but at first he'll be content just to be with you,' she
said earnestly, and was rewarded by the uncertain

look that Leigh gave her with just a hint of hope behind it.

She settled back in her seat and closed her eyes, leaving Leigh to ponder her advice, trying to remember each confrontation she had had with Bryce and exactly what he had said. Could she have been wrong about him? He'd certainly been a whole lot nicer to her since that day at the air show. Or maybe it had been her imagination because she just *wanted* him to be nicer? For a long time she argued back and forth with herself, but really it all boiled down to the fact that she just didn't know Bryce well enough to know whether he was turning on the charm or being genuine. And the only way she was going to find out was by doing as he asked and trusting him. After all, as Faye had said, she had everything to gain and nothing to lose—except peace of mind for the rest of her life, Leigh thought with a sigh that was very close to a sob.

CHAPTER SEVEN

LEIGH didn't see Bryce again until the following Sunday. She arrived early to take her charter up to Scotland and was surprised to find both Bryce and Vic Parker on the tarmac. They were both wearing white mechanics' overalls and had their heads inside the engine of the Arrow, but Bryce looked up when he heard her footsteps and jumped lightly down from the platform he was standing on. His eyes searched her face as he walked towards her, wiping his hands on a piece of clean rag. Leigh felt stupidly nervous and ill at ease, glad that he was there and yet wishing he wasn't. Looking up, she gave him a tentative smile and felt her heart leap as he immediately smiled in return.

'Good morning. All set?'

'Yes. Has my passenger arrived?'

'No.' Bryce looked at his watch. 'But he's got ten minutes yet.'

He had come up close to her and Leigh longed to reach out to him, to touch him. But aware of Vic Parker watching them, she stepped to one side and said, 'What's wrong with the Arrow?'

'Spot of engine trouble. You'll have to take the Aztec. It's all ready for you.'

Leigh strolled over to greet Vic and Bryce followed her, standing casually with his hands thrust into his pockets, chatting about the Arrow. But when Vic put his head back under the cowling,

Bryce turned to her and said, 'By the way, your passenger today especially asked for you. It seems he was very impressed with the way you flew him and some others to the races recently, and he insisted you pilot him again.' He smiled at her lazily. 'What with that and the glowing reference Faye Winter gave you, you're building up quite a name for yourself.'

Leigh laughed. 'You'd better be careful; any more compliments like that and I might ask for a rise!'

Bryce grinned, then, as he looked at her, his face changed, became intent. 'Leigh . . .'

But he had no chance to finish what he was going to say because a chauffeur-driven car drove on to the tarmac just then and pulled up alongside them. Her passenger had arrived. Leigh turned, her mind echoing Bryce's 'damn!' at the interruption, and saw that the man in the car was Mr Hollander, the racehorse owner she'd taken up to Haydock Park a couple of weeks ago.

He got out of the car and said good morning while his chauffeur got his bag of golf clubs out of the boot. Bryce took it from him and put it into the luggage compartment of the Aztec while Leigh and her passenger climbed into the cockpit. When he'd done, Bryce looked up at her from the tarmac and raised his hand in salute, his grey eyes holding hers for a long moment that set her pulses racing again.

Mr Hollander had chartered the plane to take him to play golf at Gleneagles and bring him back after dinner that evening. Very nice if you could afford it. And thank heavens there were some people who could, or she'd be out of a job, Leigh thought with a mixture of emotions. Her passenger didn't talk much during the long journey; he had a briefcase with him which he opened almost as soon as they'd taken off and he settled down to look through a sheaf of papers, sometimes making verbal notes on a miniature cassette recorder. He was dressed quite casually, in slacks and a waterproof jacket, but they were the kind of clothes that made casualness look almost elegant because of the expensiveness of the cut and material.

Leigh was glad that he didn't want to talk because it gave her more time to think of Bryce. There had been so little time together this morning, but it certainly seemed as if he had been going to say something to her—something personal, but had had no opportunity. But even so, that look he'd given her as she was about to leave had spoken volumes. Volumes, yes, but whether of love or just desire she was too unsure of herself where Bryce was concerned to tell.

She sighed, and decided that perhaps it would be better if she didn't think about him, after all. By flying the plane herself instead of putting it on auto-pilot, she was able to keep her mind off him a little, but it was tiring, so after they had refuelled at Carlisle, she sat back in her seat and let the mechanical controller take over for a while.

Mr Hollander saw her take her hands off the wheel and said, 'Er—I take it this plane is equipped with an auto-pilot?'

Leigh smiled at him reassuringly, knowing from past experience how little trust passengers had in the gadget—although they were willing enough to trust themselves to an aeroplane, which was really only another machine. 'Yes, it's very efficient and quite safe.'

He nodded and turned back to the papers on his lap while Leigh sorted out the next map she wanted. All the time they had been flying they had been passed from one radio control area to another, plotted on radar screens in stations on the ground so that their position was always known and there was always someone to contact if they got into trouble. The famous Gleneagles Hotel with its championship golf course was used to players arriving by private plane and had its own runway. As Leigh got within radio range, she called them up. 'Gleneagles tower, this is Delta Lima Bravo, good morning.'

'Good morning, Lima Bravo, go ahead.' The reply came clearly and promptly over the headset.

'Lima Bravo approaching from south-east, range fifteen miles, request joining instructions, over.'

'Lima Bravo cleared to join right base for runway zero four Q.F.E. nine nine eight milibars. Surface wind zero six zero, ten knots. Call when you have the runway in sight, over.'

A few sentences that gave Leigh all the vital information she needed to turn into the wind and glide down to the runway for a perfect three-point landing.

Mr Hollander packed away his business papers and Leigh followed him out of the plane. A caddie at once came up to take his large and heavy bag of clubs, but before he left he turned to Leigh and said, 'I've arranged for a room to be available for you if you want to rest, and you'll be served dinner at seven-thirty.'

'Why, thank you. That's extremely kind of you,' Leigh exclaimed gratefully, touched by his thoughtfulness.

But he strode off with his caddy following, hardly giving her time to thank him, to where some other men were obviously waiting for him. Presumably they would be combining both business and pleasure during their round of golf.

Leigh had never been to Gleneagles before and she took a little time to walk around the place and stretch her legs, but in the afternoon she took advantage of Mr Hollander's kindness to slip off her outer clothes and have a sleep on the bed in the room he had taken for her. At seven-thirty, as promised, a meal was brought up to her room, but it wasn't until nearly ten that she was told that Mr Hollander was ready to fly back to Shepton Ferrers.

By then it was almost dark, just the last rays of the long English spring twilight left to hold off the night, but soon even this light failed and she had to navigate by compass and by checking her direction on the radio beacons as she passed over them. Mr Hollander had gone to sit in the back of the plane for the return journey and was stretched out across the long seat at the stern, sleeping off his dinner, most likely, Leigh thought as she piloted the plane through the enclosing darkness.

After they had refuelled at Carlisle, however, he came forward and sat down beside her. 'At what height are we flying?' he enquired.

'Four thousand, five hundred feet.'

He frowned. 'I think we ought to be higher—at least five thousand, five hundred feet.'

Leigh looked at him in some surprise; he'd betrayed no sign of nervousness before.. 'This height is quite safe.'

'Nevertheless I must insist on going higher,' he replied firmly.

Leigh shrugged mentally. After all, he was paying, and flying higher wouldn't make any difference, so she might as well keep him happy. 'Very well.' She lifted the nose of the Aztec and began to climb, informing the local radio control tower as she did so. When she got to six thousand, five hundred she levelled off and pointed the new height on the altitude dial out to her passenger.

'Good. Good,' he said on a note of satisfaction. He went aft again then. Leigh heard him moving around and presently he called her name. She turned her head and saw him beckoning to her. He had a bottle of champagne and two glasses on the table in front of him. Leigh hesitated for a moment, then put the Aztec on auto-pilot, took off the headset and her safety strap and moved back down the plane towards him.

'Yes, Mr Hollander? What is it?'

'It is all right for me to open this bottle of champagne in the plane, isn't it?'

'Why, yes, of course. I don't think the cork will blow a hole through the fuselage.'

'That's good. It should go off with quite a bang at this height.'

Leigh smiled inwardly; so that was why he'd wanted to go higher!

She went to turn away, but he said, 'No, wait. I

concluded an extremely satisfactory deal this afternoon. One that should make me a millionaire all
over again,' he explained on a note of pride. 'And
something like that has to be celebrated, which is
why I brought the champagne. But I hate to drink
alone, so I want you to have a drink with me.'

Shaking her head, Leigh said with a smile, 'I'm
afraid I can't. Have you forgotten that I'm driving?'

'Just a sip will do. Come along, you must. I'm
superstitious about having someone to toast my
success with.' He'd been peeling the foil and the
wire off the bottle as he spoke and now he eased
off the cork which came out with a loud bang, the
golden liquid gushing out of the neck in a froth-
ing cascade. Hastily he whipped a champagne
flute underneath, filling up one glass and then the
other.

'There,' he said, handing the second one to her.
'Let's hope that this new deal goes off as suc-
cessfully.'

Leigh raised her glass to join in the toast, notic-
ing that it was lead crystal. Mr Hollander certainly
didn't do things by halves, she thought as she took
a token sip. It was good champagne too. She put
down the glass and began to thank him, but he put
a hand on her arm.

'Do you know what I'd like to make this day
really perfect?' he demanded, his eyes on her face,
strangely glittering and intent.

'No,' Leigh answered indulgently. 'What's that?'

He took a long swallow of the glass he was
holding and the hand holding her arm tightened.
'I'd like to join the Mile High Club.'

Leigh stared at him, so completely amazed that she couldn't speak.

'I see you know what that is.'

She knew all right. The Mile High Club had a very exclusive membership indeed; only people who'd had sex over a mile up in the air were eligible to join. So *that* was why he'd wanted to climb up to five thousand, five hundred feet!

Anger came into her face, but before she could speak, he said, 'I'm quite willing to pay for my—er—entry fee, of course. I'm sure you could use five hundred pounds.'

'You're crazy!' Leigh exclaimed furiously, her face hot with embarrassment.

'All right—a thousand, then.'

'Is that why you insisted that I fly you?' Leigh demanded. 'So that you could try this on?' She saw by his face that it was, and went on angrily, 'Well, you've just been wasting your time, because I'm not interested in your—your proposition.'

'So name your price,' he said, still sure of himself.

'I don't have a price. I'm not for sale.'

'Nonsense, everyone has a price.' His tone was rougher now and he still had hold of her arm.

'Well, that's where you're wrong.' Leigh tried to pull away, but his grip tightened. The first awareness of danger came to her and she tried to speak authoritatively as she said, 'Please let go of my arm and return to your seat. I have to make a radio check.'

'You'll have plenty of time for that later,' he told her as he pulled her roughly against him. 'I've told you that I want you, and I always get what I want.'

'Let go of me! I have to fly the plane.'

But her words were cut off as he tried to kiss her. Leigh could smell alcohol on his breath and realised too late that he'd probably been drinking most of the day. Terror gripped her and she began to fight him off in earnest, hitting out at him with her fists and trying to knee him. But there was little space in the confined limits of the cabin and he was much, much stronger than she was. The ribbon came out of her hair and it swirled about her head so that she could hardly see. He managed to grasp one of her wrists and began to bend her back across the stern seats. Desperately, her breath coming in sobbing pants, Leigh raised her free hand and raked her nails across his cheek. He swore viciously and hit her across the face with the back of his hand, the ring he wore cutting her near her ear and drawing blood.

He hit her with such force that she fell, banging her head on the base of one of the seats as she did so. For a moment everything went black and she was too stunned to move, but then she felt his hands on her clothes, lifting her skirt, and she kicked out convulsively. She must have made contact somewhere, because she heard him grunt and swear again, but she immediately turned over on to her front and began to struggle away from him up the gangway towards the controls. He grabbed her legs, but Leigh clung to the base of one of the seats, trying to pull herself forward, sobbing and more terrified than she'd ever been in her life.

Hollander caught hold of her blouse, but somehow she managed to get a purchase on something with her foot and pulled herself forward a few more inches, desperately reaching out towards the control panel. The auto-pilot buttons were at the base of the vertical section of the 'T' shape formed by the controls, near the floor. If only she could reach them . . . The silky material of her blouse tore down to her waist. His hands were on her again and she could hear his heavy, erratic breathing as he got to his knees and bent over her. With a last, fear-driven surge of strength, Leigh flung her arms up and forward and her fingers touched the buttons. Almost at once he began to drag her back down the gangway, but there had been time. She'd managed to press the buttons.

Angry but triumphant, Hollander turned her over, using her roughly. Her skirt was round her waist from being dragged along the floor and now he began to tear off what was left of her blouse. For a couple of minutes nothing discernible happened to the plane, but then the nose went down and it began to dive.

'Let go of me or we'll both be killed!' Leigh yelled at him. 'Do you hear me? The plane's going to crash!' For a heart-stopping moment she thought that he was too far gone with lust to hear, but as the angle of the plane began to tip towards the vertical the crazed look left his eyes to be replaced by one of fear.

'You bitch!' he snarled at her. 'Go and pull it up.'

He let her get up and Leigh staggered into the pilot's seat, pulling back on the yoke and using flaps and throttle to bring her out of the drive, glad now that she had the extra two thousand feet in which to level out. But the danger wasn't over yet. Hollander came up behind her and put a hand on her shoulder, pressing so hard that he hurt her.

'Put it back on auto-pilot. Do as I say!' he yelled at her.

Cringing under his grip, Leigh slammed on right yoke and rudder and sent him smashing into the side of the plane as it banked steeply.

'I shouldn't do that if I were you,' she snapped out shortly. 'You just might live to regret it.'

He bellowed furiously and came at her again, so this time she pulled back on the yoke and the Aztec's nose lifted into a steep climb, making him grab the back of the seats to stop himself tumbling down to the stern. Behind her she heard the champagne bottle and glasses crash to the floor and smash on the carpet, filling the cabin with the smell of wine. Glancing over her shoulder, she saw that he hadn't yet given up, was still on his feet, his eyes murderous. But there was no way, now that she had this beautiful weapon in her hands, that he was going to win. Fastening her safety strap, Leigh put the Aztec through some manoeuvres that no self-respecting pilot would ever do with a passenger on board, and she didn't stop until the ghastly stench of sickness reached her nostrils. The drink that he had consumed that day, plus the buffetting she'd put him through, had proved too much for Hollander's stomach. He had pulled himself into a seat and was lying back in it, groaning miserably, even his curses stopped now.

Satisfied that he wouldn't give her any more trouble, Leigh settled on an even course and pushed the throttle open until it came up against the stops. Dazedly she pushed her hair away from her eyes and tried to take stock of the situation. Blood was still dripping down from the cut on her face and her left eye felt sore and puffy where she had hit it on the seat base. Her lower lip, too, felt bruised where Hollander had hit her. She began to shiver and reached up for her jacket, putting it on over the shreds of her blouse, but still her body shook and her teeth chattered as waves of shock ran through her. She fought to control it, her hands gripping the control yoke fiercely, flying the plane by the most direct route and at maximum speed, longing to be safe on the ground, among other people.

As soon as they were within radio distance of Shepton Ferrers, she called up the tower and asked them to get in touch with Bryce or Vic Parker and have them standing by on the runway.

A few minutes later they called her back. 'Have passed on your message, Lima Bravo. Mr Allerton wants to know if there's any trouble with the plane?'

Leigh looked over her shoulder to where Hollander was slumped in his seat, muttering bitterly to himself. 'No,' she answered the tower. 'Just tell him it's some trouble with the—er—cargo.'

Her landing that night was one of the worst she'd ever made. She had no strength left to fly it and just drove the poor Aztec on to the runway, too fast and without enough energy in her legs for the toe-brakes. They bounced along and somehow managed to come to a halt before the runway ran out. Leigh could feel the muscles in her arms jerking as she tried to pull back on the throttle and the scream of the engines matched the screaming in her head. At the end of the runway she gave up; there was just no way she could turn the plane and taxi it over to the hangar. The engine stalled and she didn't even switch it off, just sat there with her head in her hands.

It could only have been a couple of minutes later that the door was wrenched open from the outside. Bryce put his head in, his voice sharp with anxiety. 'What's happened?' Then the sickness stench hit him and he saw her face in the muted glow of the cockpit light. 'Dear God!'

He was beside her in a moment, unfastening the straps and gently lifting her out of her seat and passing her down to Vic, who was waiting below. Greedily Leigh sucked in the fresh, clean air of early morning, letting it clear some of the stuffiness out of her brain. Vic carried her over to the grass and pulled off his jacket for her to sit on. Bryce stayed in the plane a moment longer and then came over to them, his face grim.

'What the hell happened?' Vic asked him.

'From the look of it, Leigh had to fight him off,' Bryce said furiously. 'The stinking swine!' He dropped down to his knees beside her. 'Is that what happened, Leigh?'

She gulped and nodded. 'Oh, Bryce, I'm so sorry about the plane. It's in a terrible mess. But I had to make him ill to keep him away from me.'

'For God's sake, what does the plane matter?' Bryce exclaimed, his voice rough. 'Did he . . .? Did you manage to . . .?'

'I'm all right,' Leigh told him tiredly.

Very gently his hand went to her chin and he

turned her face so that he could see it clearly in the runway lights. He cursed violently. 'The filthy swine!'

Getting up, he went back into the plane and she saw him pull Hollander to the door and literally kick him out on to the ground, then jump down after him and almost drag him over to his Jaguar, which was parked nearby. He slammed the door on the man and came over to them again.

'Vic, will you taxi the plane back to the hangar? I'm going to take Leigh down to the police station so that she can . . .'

'No,' Leigh cut in quickly. She began to struggle to her feet and both men immediately reached down to help her up, but it was Bryce who kept his arm round her. 'I don't want to tell the police.'

'But why not? You can't let that swine get away with it,' Bryce said hotly.

'He didn't get away with it—I gave him quite a rough time up there once I got control of the plane again.' She looked at him pleadingly as Vic walked away and left them alone. 'Please, Bryce, I know you're angry; I was too at first, but I've had a little time to think. If we go to the police there's bound to be publicity. After all, it isn't exactly a common occurrence in a plane, is it, for a man to try and— to try and . . .' She stopped, unable to say the word, her body starting to shake again.

Bryce's arms came round her and she un- ashamedly leaned against him, taking comfort from his strength. 'Don't think about it. You're still in shock.'

'No, I'm all right, just a bit shaken.' Raising her head, she said, 'Really there's been no great harm done, except to the plane, and I know you're furious about that, but honestly, Bryce, the publicity wouldn't do Allerton's any good.'

'Do you think that's all I care about—the plane?' he demanded, his voice raw.

His face was half in light, half in shadow, but she could see the twisted, bitter look about his mouth. Slowly she lifted her hand and gently smoothed his lips with her fingertip. 'No. I think you're angry about what he did to me, too. But please try to understand that that kind of publicity will only hurt me more.'

He was silent for a moment, then said, 'All right, if that's the way you want it. But he needn't think he's going to get away with it entirely,' he added grimly. He realised that she was shivering again. 'You're trembling. Come on, I'll take you home.'

Hollander was sitting in the back of the car and immediately began to speak when Bryce unlocked it and they got in. He had evidently fully recovered from his air sickness, but he was full of fear, gabbling almost as he begged them not to go to the police, offering to pay for any damage that had been done, make compensation, anything.

'Oh, you'll pay all right,' Bryce told him viciously. When they pulled up outside Allerton's he ordered Leigh to stay where she was and pulled Hollander out of the car and round the side of the building. The man was babbling with fear and Leigh almost felt sorry for him as she saw the purposeful way Bryce dragged him out of sight.

When he came back about five minutes later he

was alone and he was flexing his knuckles as if he'd hit something very hard. 'Now, let's get you home.'

'What did you do with him?' Leigh asked as Bryce drove out of the airport.

'Left him in the tender hands of his chauffeur— after I'd made sure that he'll remember tonight for quite some time to come. And tomorrow I'll slap him with a bill for damages that will make his hair curl,' he added with grim relish.

He drove on through the night, heading towards town. Leigh leaned back against the head-rest, her eyes half closed, tired but strangely content. Then she dimly became aware of the lights at a road junction and exclaimed, 'Hey, you're going the wrong way!'

'This is the way to the hotel.'

'But I don't live there any more. I moved out a couple of weeks ago. I'm renting a cottage at Little Marsden now.'

They had only gone a few yards out of their way and Bryce was able to back up and take the right road.

'I didn't know you'd moved,' he commented.

'I told Carol.'

'But she obviously didn't see fit to pass on the information,' he replied dryly.

The village was in complete darkness as they drove up. They closed the doors of the car quietly and Bryce helped her up the garden path. Leigh fumbled with the key and he took it from her and let them in. By this time she was shaking again, but from cold as much as anything.

'You need a hot drink,' Bryce told her. 'Go on

upstairs and get ready for bed and I'll bring it up to you.'

Leigh turned to obey him, too tired and shaken to even consider any double meaning to that remark. Going into the bathroom, she cleaned her face as best she could and grimaced at her reflection; it would be a couple of days before she looked human again. She put on a clean nightie and was glad that she'd left the bedroom tidy before she went out that morning. Bryce came in just as she was putting her skirt and jacket on a hanger.

'Here, I'll do that for you.' He set down the tray he was carrying and took the things from her. 'Come on, get into bed. I've made you cocoa. I didn't know whether you took sugar or not, so I brought it up. And I also . . .' his voice slowed and Leigh glanced up to see that he was staring into the wardrobe where the clothes that Don's son had left behind were hanging, '. . . brought up some aspirins for you to take,' he finished, his voice sounding quite different. He hung up her suit and closed the wardrobe quickly as if he wanted to shut the men's clothes out of his mind.

Leigh got into bed and he put the tray on her lap. 'You'd better tell me exactly what happened,' he said abruptly.

Leigh did so, her voice quite steady until she reached the part where she had almost failed to fight Hollander off, and then another tremor of shock ran through her so that the mug shook in her hands.

Bryce took it and the tray from her and put them on the floor. 'It's all right, Leigh, it's over. You're safe now, darling.' His arms went round her and she turned into them.

'Hold me. Please hold me,' she whispered.

'Oh, Leigh, my darling girl!' He drew her closer, his arms tightening. 'Oh, God, if you only knew how much I want to kiss you, love you,' he groaned. 'Why did this have to happen tonight when your poor face stops me from showing you just how crazy I am about you?'

But even so he didn't do at all badly, kissing her neck, her throat, her ears, all the parts of her face where she wasn't hurt, and oh, so very gently around her poor bruised eye and lip.

His mouth against her neck he breathed, 'Oh, Leigh, my dearest! Get well quickly. There's so much I want to say to you.' He straightened up and looked down at her as she lay back on the pillow, gently stroking her hair off her face. 'But tonight isn't the time. You're tired and I ought to leave you alone. And, remember, I don't want to see you at work until you're better.'

'But what about my runs tomorrow?' Leigh protested.

'Stop worrying—I'll fly them. Now go to sleep.' He bent and kissed her lightly on the forehead.

'I ought to come down and bolt the door after you.'

'No need. I'll sleep in a chair downstairs until the morning, in case you wake and need anything. I'll let myself out in the morning.'

'You don't have to do that.'

'I want to,' he answered, picking up her hand and kissing her fingers one by one.

Leigh smiled. 'The neighbours will think I've got

a lover if they see you leave in the morning!'

His hold on her hand tightened convulsively, then he stood up. 'Call me if you need anything.'

He moved towards the door, but Leigh stopped him. 'Bryce!'

'Yes?'

'Those clothes in the wardrobe belong to Don Chapman's son.'

'Don's son?' He stared at her in surprise.

'Yes. I suppose you'd call him my landlord, although I've never met him. But it was Don who let me rent this cottage from him while his son is away in America.'

Bryce came back and leant over her, putting one hand on either side of her pillow. 'Remind me to spank you some time!'

Leigh's eyes opened wide in feigned innocence. 'Why, what have I done wrong?'

'You could have told me who those clothes belonged to the minute I saw them.'

'But why should I?'

'Because it was the only thing that held me back from telling you just how much I loved you.'

Then he was gone, turning to blow her a mocking kiss in the doorway before flicking off the light, leaving her staring after him in the darkness.

CHAPTER EIGHT

IT was late before Leigh got up the next morning. She wandered downstairs in her dressing-gown and saw the indentation that Bryce's head had made in the cushion that he'd used as a pillow on the settee. It could hardly have been very comfortable, the settee was only about five feet long and Bryce was a good six feet. Leigh sat on the settee and picked up the cushion, holding it up to her face, the faint tang of his aftershave still lingering to make her heart beat faster.

He phoned her later that day, between flights and dealing with the management side as well. He asked her how she was, but there was little time for endearments. 'I'm afraid I won't be able to see you until Wednesday,' he told her. 'The Aztec will take a few days to clean up and re-carpet, so I'm driving over to Coventry tonight with Vic to borrow a plane from a friend, so that we can meet all our charter agreements. And tomorrow I'm taking your run over to Le Touquet—that was an overnight job, if you remember?'

'Can't anyone else take it?' she asked wistfully.

She could almost hear him smile over the phone. ''Fraid not, darling. We'll just have to look forward to Wednesday. I'll get back as soon as I can and then I'll come over for you.'

Leigh wasn't altogether sorry; even though she longed to see him, she was feminine enough to want

him to see her at her best, and by Wednesday perhaps her face would be better, her lip had started
to go down already.

So she bore the wait as patiently as she could
and on Wednesday morning her lip was completely
better, the bruise by her eye she was able to cover
by make-up, and if she let her hair down you
couldn't see the scratch near her ear. But the ex-
citement and anticipation built up unbearably that
day and in the afternoon she was so restless that
she couldn't sit still for more than two minutes,
continually looking at the clock, and getting up to
pace about the room, longing for the phone to ring
and willing herself not to phone up the office to
find out what time Bryce was due in because she
was afraid that Carol would answer the phone and
put two and two together.

It did ring, eventually, at about five o'clock, and
Leigh snatched up the receiver. 'Yes? Hello.'

'Leigh? This is Don Chapman. We got back from
America this morning and I thought I'd give you a
ring to see how you were.'

'I'm fine, thanks. Oh—and so is the cottage.'

'Good. I was worried about you, the others tell
me you haven't been in to work this week.'

'No, but I'm all right, really. I'll be back tomorrow. Are you at Allerton's now?'

'Yes. Came in to find out if I was down for any
runs this week.'

'Don, could you do something for me, please,'
Leigh said eagerly. 'Will you find out Bryce's
E.T.A.?'

'Don't have to,' he replied promptly. 'He flew in
about twenty minutes ago. In an all-fired hurry,

too—just had a quick word and then dashed off home.'

'Oh, I see.' Leigh almost laughed with happiness over the phone, picturing Bryce hurrying to go home and change, not even bothering to phone so that he could meet her that much more quickly. 'Thanks a lot, Don. See you. 'Bye!'

She put down the receiver over Don's surprised voice and ran to pick up her bag. It would take Bryce some time to get home and change and in that time she could drive over to his flat and they would be together that much sooner. Only after she was driving along in the car did it occur to Leigh that she should have phoned first, that they might pass each other on the way. So she kept an anxious eye out for his car, but no Jaguar went speeding by in the other direction, and she laughed at her fears when she saw his car parked outside his block of flats. She took the lift up to his floor, her heart beating loudly, her body already tingling with anticipation at the thought of his touch. Finding his door, Leigh rang the bell, waited for a few moments, then rang it long and loudly again when he didn't come straightaway. It was a solid door with one of those peephole gadgets set into it. Leigh thought she saw a movement through it and waited impatiently, her eyes brilliant with love and expectation. A minute later the door opened wide.

'Oh, hallo, Leigh. You certainly picked your moment to call!'

Carol stood in the doorway, an amused, insolent smile on her face. Her blonde hair was tousled and the dress she was wearing was unbuttoned to the waist, as if it had been put on hurriedly, and it was clear that she had no bra on underneath. Leigh stared at her, taking in her dishevelled state, her bare feet. Then a door inside the flat opened and Leigh looked past her. The front door opened straight into the sitting-room. Bryce came into it from another room, and he was wearing nothing but a bathrobe!

Leigh's face drained completely of colour. She took one look at him, then turned and ran.

'Leigh! Leigh, wait!'

She heard him call her but didn't stop. She didn't wait for the lift but took the stairs, running down them two or three at a time, regardless of the danger of falling. She didn't realise she was crying until she got in the car and began to drive away, and had to brush the tears from her eyes so that she could see. Leigh drove for miles, completely unaware of where she was or in what direction she was heading, until some time later she saw a track leading on to a common and pulled up at the end of it. There was a lovely view over the countryside, but she didn't see it, she just sat huddled in her seat and gave way to unhappiness. At last she cried herself out and fell asleep, uncomfortably lying back in the seat of the little car.

When she awoke, Leigh felt stiff and cold. She rubbed her arms to bring the circulation back and saw that it was almost five in the morning. Drearily she started the car and backed down the track on to the road, realising that she had no idea where she was. For some time she drove about just trying to get her bearings, then luckily found a signpost that headed in the right direction and followed it, her head aching, longing to get home. But she'd

been driving about for so long that the petrol
warning light on the dashboard started to flash and
she had to stop and ask a milkman on his round
where the nearest open garage was. The only one
he knew of was in the next town, some miles away,
so she had to turn off her route and head for it.

She almost made it, getting to within a mile of
the garage before the Mini ran dry. Luckily Leigh
had a spare petrol can in the boot, so she was able
to walk to the garage to fill it. But the delay meant
that she didn't get back to the cottage until nearly
seven. She quickly showered, changed and had a
slice of toast, then sat down at the table and wrote
a letter of resignation to Allerton's.

The day was hot and sunny as Leigh parked
outside the office. She was wearing just a short-
sleeved white blouse and maroon pleated skirt,
sunglasses over her eyes again and her hair brushed
neatly back. She walked into Reception ready to
face Carol's triumphant smile, but she wasn't there.
In her place stood a pleasant-looking middle-aged
woman who smiled at her as she came in.

Leigh hesitated for a moment, then handed her
the envelope containing her resignation letter.
'Would you see that Mr Allerton gets this, please?'

'Yes, of course. Are you Miss Bishop?'

'Yes.'

'Well, Mr Allerton would like to see you. He
told me to ask you to go to his office the minute
you came in.'

'Did he?' Leigh commented dryly, and turned in
the opposite direction and went through to the
crew room.

Don was there with a couple of the other pilots,

but she fobbed off their questions about her being away from work by saying that she'd had a cold and went over to look at the work roster. She had been put down to pick up some passengers at Gatwick at ten-thirty and fly them over to Cardiff, then on to Coventry and back to Gatwick again. Immediately she looked at the latest weather report, then sat down to file her flight plan. She had only been sitting there a few minutes when Bryce strode in, her letter in his hands.

He came straight over to her and said harshly, 'Will you come up to my office, Leigh? I want to speak to you.'

Leigh glanced up at him. There was a dark, tired look about his eyes and he needed a shave. 'I have nothing to say to you,' she replied coldly.

He leaned forward, lowering his voice. 'Will you at least let me explain . . .'

'No. I'm not interested.'

'Leigh, please!' His hand came out and clasped her wrist urgently.

Her green eyes flashed fire. 'Don't you dare touch me!' she hissed at him.

Bryce stared down at her, his eyes growing bleak as he released her wrist. 'Where did you go last night?'

'What's that got to do with you?' she retorted icily.

'Only that I waited outside your house all night until six-thirty this morning, for you to come home.'

'Really?' Leigh answered disdainfully. 'I'm surprised you wasted your time when you could have been making it with Carol—or one of your other, many women!'

Bryce flinched as if she'd hit him, the muscles in his jaw tightening and his features setting into a frozen mask. He turned and became aware of the others staring at them. Looking at Don, he said coldly, 'I want to speak to you,' and walked out of the room.

Leigh bent her head to her work, not looking up as Don followed Bryce out. The air of the room was still charged, electric, and she knew that the other pilots were agog with curiosity, longing for her to go so that they could discuss what had happened. Hastily she finished her flight plan and hurried out on to the tarmac, glad to get out into the open. She was taking the Arrow today and Vic had it all ready for her. He started asking her how she was, but to his surprise she cut him off rather brusquely and climbed into the plane, taking off as soon as she had clearance, even though she was too early.

The day passed, as even the worst days must pass, but Leigh didn't go straight home to the cottage because she was afraid Bryce might follow her there, so instead she went into Shepton Ferrers and had a meal and then went to the cinema and watched a film that was just moving shapes on a screen, so little did she concentrate on it.

Bryce was away on business the next day so there was no danger of running into him, but the news of their row had spread and the atmosphere in the crew room was alive with interest and speculation. The fact that Carol seemed to have left and been replaced was also adding to the rumours and conjecture. No one actually said anything to Leigh or asked her any questions, but she could tell from the way the conversation abruptly stopped whenever she walked into the room that the other pilots were talking about her, and Mike, especially, looked more than a little amused.

Only Don made a point of speaking to her directly. 'I tried to phone you last night, but you were out. My wife wants you to come and have dinner with us—tonight if that's okay.' He saw Leigh hesitate and added, 'She wants to try out making some American dishes and needs a guinea pig, only she says I won't do because whatever she cooks I always just say, "Very nice, dear," out of habit.'

Leigh laughed and accepted, glad of an excuse to keep her away from the cottage that night.

But after they'd eaten that evening, Don's wife made an excuse to leave them alone together in the sitting-room and she found that Don had had an ulterior motive in inviting her.

Looking slightly embarrassed, he drew on his pipe and said, 'I'm afraid I—er—I rather misled you when you first came here.' Leigh looked at him enquiringly and he went on, 'Something I said to you, quite unintentionally, of course, seems to have given you the wrong impression. About Bryce.'

Leigh's face whitened and she looked away. 'I'm really not interested in Bryce,' she observed coldly.

'Well, interested or not, he's asked me to put the record straight. And to do that I'll have to tell you the whole story of that affair you thought Bryce had had.'

Her face tense, Leigh said shortly, 'I don't want to hear.'

'But you're going to hear,' Don said forcibly. 'That affair wasn't between Bryce and the pilot's wife at all.'

Leigh's head came up. 'But you said . . .'

'No, I only said that the wife came down here to see Bryce. Let me explain: we sometimes get girls, mostly pupils from the flying school, who hang around hoping to be taken up for a flight. Well, this particular pilot got very friendly with one of those girls and started having an affair with her. Eventually of course the wife found out and she came down here to see Bryce. He had the pilot up into his office and there was this unholy row which ended when Bryce told the pilot in no uncertain terms to sort himself out. And of course he chose his wife and they moved away from temptation. And since then Bryce has come down like a ton of bricks on any girls he's found hanging around.'

Well, that last was certainly true; Leigh remembered the way he'd gone off at her the first time she'd met him, on the tarmac, when he thought she was hanging around for a joy-ride. But the rest? She looked at Don uncertainly, wondering if Bryce had put him up to this, then dismissed the thought, sure that Don would never lie to her. If he said it was so, then it must be.

But even so, she shook her head. 'It doesn't make any difference. I'm leaving Allerton's as soon as I've worked out my notice. Bryce means nothing to me.'

Immediately Don lost his usual placidity and exploded into anger. 'My God, girl, have you looked at yourself in the mirror? You look like death! And Bryce is the same. You two need your heads banging together! You're just a couple of lovesick fools who are punishing yourselves by your own pride—and all because of a stupid mis-understanding.'

'I'm not in love with him,' Leigh protested defensively.

Don smiled thinly. 'Then you're certainly giving a good imitation! One only has to take a look at your face to know you're eating your heart out for the man.' He leaned forward persuasively. 'There's no room for pride where love's concerned, Leigh. If you want him, go and get him.'

Leigh looked at him for a long moment. She knew he was trying to be kind but he didn't know about Carol. Standing up she said politely, 'Thank you for explaining and trying to help, but you're wrong—I don't want him.'

Bryce was back the next day. He must have spoken to Don, because he came quite eagerly into the crew room, his eyes seeking her out as she stood by the coffee machine. Leigh looked up and their eyes met and held. Then she deliberately turned her back on him. Behind her she heard the door slam shut as he strode away.

Leigh was infinitely glad when Saturday came round. She had only one flight that day, to take a businessman up to Newcastle and return empty. Except that the weather changed as she travelled north becoming dark and cloudy, the trip up was uneventful. She dropped her passenger, had a snack and started back, but by now the clouds had evil greyish-purple centres. Cu-nims, pilots called them; anvil-shaped cumulo-nimbus clouds inside which all hell can break loose, for they contained vertical rushing air currents that could lift and drop even a large airliner like a yoyo. And if that wasn't enough they could contain rain, hail and lightning. In severe storms it had even been known for the hailstones to be so big that they had damaged the fuselage of aircraft.

It was a phenomenon that Leigh had encountered many times before and she wasn't afraid of it, but it was very tiring having to fly round the storm, avoiding even the medium-sized clouds that could do her no harm, because they sometimes masked a dangerous one just behind. Soon her head began to ache and she longed for a couple of aspirins. And she was very tired; she had been sleeping badly ever since Wednesday, unable to fall asleep until she reached the point of exhaustion, and then waking only a couple of hours later to lie tossing and turning, trying not to think of Bryce, but her thoughts always full of him, even if it was only how much she despised him.

She wiped a weary hand across her brow, and altered course yet again to avoid another cloud. Whoever said falling in love is the most wonderful feeling in the world must be mad, she thought grimly. Being in love is hell! No, amend that: being in love with the wrong man is hell. As she travelled south the storm passed, but it left behind it a grey overcast sky. Leigh climbed above it and flew on at four thousand feet. With a sigh of relief she came within range of Shepton Ferrers tower and called them up, asking for weather conditions and permission to land.

'Cloud has spread in from the south-west,' Control informed her. 'Now eight eighths cover, base sixteen hundred feet, tops three thousand five hundred.'

'Thank you, Shepton tower. Weather copied.'

She did her pre-landing checks and then lowered the nose of the plane to fly through the thick grey cottonwool murkiness that covered the earth. Three thousand feet, two thousand. Leigh came out of the clouds at sixteen hundred feet, dead on course, and saw the airfield spread out below her. At the same instant she saw a movement in the sky to her left and realised that there was something else in the air only a few yards away. In one reflexive movement she slammed on the right rudder and banked the plane steeply, at the same time diving downwards. For a fraction of a second the cockpit seemed to be filled with bright colours and she realised that the other craft was a microlight, one of the powered hang-gliders with wings more jewel-bright than a butterfly's. The flier's terrified face came into sight for an instant and then was gone as the Arrow plunged away.

Oh, God, let me miss him! Let me miss him! Time seemed to stand still as Leigh frantically listened to the sound of the plane, waiting for any unusual bump or scraping noise. For a moment she thought she was clear, but her undercarriage was down and she thought she felt something grate against the wheels. Oh, God, no!

But the earth was hurtling fast towards her and she had only time to think of levelling out of the mad dive. Somehow she pulled up the nose and straightened up, her right wing only a few feet off the runway. She climbed again, circling, looking round the sky for the glider, petrified with fear. Then she saw him. He was going down in strange, jerking loops, the shape of the sail looking different somehow, out of line on one side, but at least he wasn't just plummetting into the ground. Leigh could see people and emergency vehicles beginning to race across the airfield towards where he would land. It might be survivable. It just might be survivable! Turning the plane, she lined up with the runway and came in to land again.

The moment the Arrow came to a stop she turned off the engine and jumped down on to the runway, almost falling because all the strength seemed to have gone out of her legs. Picking herself up, she began to run across the grass to where a crowd of people and cars were converging on the gay colours on the grass. She had almost reached it when someone grabbed hold of her and made her stop.

Bryce's voice said urgently, 'No, Leigh. Wait!' but she tried to fight him off.

'I've got to know. I've got to know!' She beat her fists against his chest as he held her, her voice high and hysterical with fear.

Calling out over his shoulder, Bryce yelled to Vic Parker, 'For God's sake go and find out!' But he wouldn't let Leigh go, holding her tightly pinned within his arms despite her struggles.

It seemed an age before Vic pushed his way through the crowd and then started to run back to them. Leigh turned to look at him, her heart cold with dread.

'He's all right,' Vic shouted. 'He's all right!'

Leigh let out a great, gasping breath and collapsed against Bryce, hardly hearing Vic as he went on breathlessly, 'His sail just caught your wheel and all he's got is a twisted ankle from landing heavily. Serve him damn well right, too,' he added feelingly. 'Those microlights are supposed to keep to their own circuit of the airfield, away from the runway. He could have killed you both if you hadn't reacted so quickly.'

But Leigh wasn't listening, she had her head buried against Bryce's shoulder and was sobbing in relief. He let her cry for a few minutes, his hand gently stroking her hair, but then some people realised who she was and began to gather round and he led her back towards the airport buildings, his arms still round her.

Airfields were always busy on Saturdays, and everyone in it seemed to be trying to look at her. Leigh kept her head buried on Bryce's shoulder and thankfully let him take over. He took her into his office and sat her down. Vic followed him in, as did a couple of the other pilots.

'Go and get her a coffee,' Bryce ordered. He handed her a handkerchief and she wiped her face.

'I'm all right, really.'

'Oh, sure. That's why you're shaking like a leaf.' Somebody brought a plastic mug of coffee and Bryce took it and held it out to her. 'Come on, darling, drink this. It will make you feel a whole lot better.'

It did, but the fact that he'd called her darling and the way he was looking at her helped a great deal more.

'Bryce . . .'

He smiled and put a finger on her lips to silence her. Someone came into the room asking for him and he moved away, but was back a few moments later with a short, grey-haired man beside him. 'Leigh, this is the Airfield Manager, Mr Claydon. He'll have to make a statement to the authorities about what's happened and he has to ask you some questions.'

'Yes, all right,' Leigh agreed tonelessly. She looked up and saw that everyone else was leaving. 'Will you—will you stay with me?'

'Yes, of course,' Bryce answered at once, his tone warm.

The manager asked the questions matter-of-factly and Leigh answered as best she could, giving speed, position, height, all the details that he wanted. Then he asked her to write out a statement of what had happened. She tried, but her hand was shaking so much she couldn't hold a pen, so she had to dictate it to Bryce and then sign it.

When Mr Claydon had gone, Leigh sat silently in the chair, her hands clasped together in front of her on the desk, her eyes mirroring her emotions as she remembered the shock and terror of the near accident. In a small, frightened voice, she asked, 'What's going to happen?'

'The Civil Aviation Authority will have to hold an enquiry, of course. But you know that; it's automatic whenever there's an accident or a near miss.'

'Will I lose my licence?'

'Why should you?' Bryce asked brusquely. 'It wasn't your fault.'

Slowly Leigh shook her head. 'I was so tired. If

I'd reacted quicker I might have missed him completely.'

Immediately Bryce came round the desk and took hold of her hands. He saw the desperate appeal in her dark-shadowed eyes and spoke with forceful insistence. 'Leigh, you know as well as I do that those powered hang-gliders are a menace to aircraft. Sooner or later an accident like this was bound to happen. That chap was in the wrong place and he's damn lucky that you had such split-second reactions or he'd have dropped out of the sky like a stone.' His hands tightened on hers. 'Darling, there was no way you could have known he was there. Those microlights don't show up on radar and he was high enough to have been in the cloud, so the control tower didn't see him when you asked for landing clearance. He probably lost himself in the cloud and came down out of it a few moments before you did and found himself right in line with the runway. But it was definitely his fault; he should never have been there.'

Leigh gave a little nod. Her hands tightened on his for a moment, then she took them away and held them clasped in her lap. Bryce straightened up, a frown of anger on his face. 'Perhaps this will force the authorities to bring in some sort of law to govern the activities of hang-gliders,' he said forcefully. 'There are so many of them now that they're become a real menace. It's a cheap way to go flying, I suppose, but most of those chaps know nothing about navigation or air regulations. They're a danger to themselves and everyone else. They ought to be made to take a test and get a licence to fly, the same way that a pilot does.'

He was pacing up and down, his voice heated, but he broke off when he saw that Leigh wasn't listening. 'Sorry, darling,' he said ruefully as he came to sit on the edge of the desk beside her, 'I'm afraid this is something I feel strongly about, and after what's happened today I'm certainly going to do my utmost to make sure some sort of legislation is passed. But don't worry,' he added reassuringly, 'I won't let them suspend your licence.'

Leigh sat back wearily in her seat. 'It doesn't matter anyway. I'm leaving here and I might just as well go now.'

His jaw tightening, Bryce said roughly, 'You're not leaving, Leigh. And you know it.'

Holding her hands tightly together, she said firmly, 'Yes, I am. I won't come back after today.'

Bryce stood looking down at her for a long moment, then said briskly, 'Come on, up you get!'

Slowly Leigh pushed herself to her feet. 'Would you—do you think someone would mind driving me home?'

'Certainly I'll drive you home. But not yet. First you're going to take the Arrow up again.'

'No!' Leigh immediately recoiled, but he gripped her arm firmly and propelled her towards the door.

'Oh, yes, you are. If you don't go up straight-away you'll lose your nerve.'

'No, I don't want to Bryce, please. I'll take it up tomorrow.'

'Tomorrow won't do. It has to be now.'

'But I can't!' There was panic in her voice as she tried to pull back.

'Yes, you can. Come on.'

He half dragged her out into the open. Someone

had taxied the Arrow over to the hangar and it
stood waiting. Leigh tried to shake him off, pleaded
with him, but Bryce wouldn't take no for an
answer. He bundled her into the cockpit and
fastened the seat-belt round her, plonked the headset on her head.

'Now, take her up,' he comm inded.

Leigh stared at the controls, her earlier terror
coming back to her so strongly that she could
almost smell the fear. She turned to Lim, her face
ashen. 'Bryce, I just can't. I can still see his face!
He was so close that I could see his face. And the
bright colours. The light shining through the
colours.' She buried her head in her hands, pushing
her fists into her eyes to try and shut out the mental
pictures.

'Yes, you can, love.' Bryce reached out and
pulled her hands down, holding them reassuringly,
his eyes dark and intent. For the second time he
said to her, 'Trust me, Leigh.'

She looked into his face for a long, long moment.
What she read there made her give a small sigh
and then she turned to put her hands on the control
yoke. 'Shepton tower, this is Delta Lima Hotel
Whisky Bravo, pre-flight check and request taxi.'

Bryce smiled at her, his eyes aflame with love.
'That's my girl!'

They had been flying for about twenty minutes
when Leigh put the plane on auto-pilot and took
off her headset, switching over to the cabin micro-
phone. She turned to Bryce and smiled. 'Despot!'
she mocked him.

He grinned. 'That sounds much more like your
old self. Now, woman, come here,' he added, pul-

ling her to him and kissing her in a very business-like manner.

It was some time before he raised his head and his voice was unsteady as he said, 'You were quite wrong about Carol, you know. That day when you saw her at my place, I'd been in such a darn hurry to get home and change so that I could meet you that I forgot about the letters waiting for me to sign. I was in the middle of having a shower when she arrived, bringing the letters, so I told her to wait. I'd just started to dress when you turned up and immediately jumped to the wrong conclusion,' he added only half mockingly.

'But Carol *looked* as if she'd been making love,' Leigh pointed out. 'Her dress was undone and she didn't have any shoes on.'

Grimly he said, 'Yes, I noticed that too. And that's why you won't be seeing her around any more. She obviously guessed that there was something between us and decided to use that ploy to try and break us up. It damn nearly worked, too. But the moment I realised what she'd done, I told her to get out, she'd created enough trouble.'

'I suppose she fancied you,' Leigh commented dryly.

He grinned smugly. 'Can I help it if women find me so damnably attractive?'

Leigh hit him on the jaw with her bunched fist. 'Pig! I can see I'll have to cut you down to size!'

His face grew serious. 'Oh, but you've done that several times already. When you got the wrong end of the stick about me from Don and wouldn't believe me when I said it wasn't true.'

'But Mike did corroborate that, you know.'

'Mike would,' Bryce answered shortly. 'Just out of perverseness, and especially if he thought it would give him a chance of cutting me out when he wanted you himself.'

'I don't see why he should have thought that you fancied me, though,' Leigh commented. 'After all, Carol was available and she's very curvy and very blonde, whereas . . .'

'Whereas from the moment I met you I suddenly realised how much I prefer skinny birds with brown hair and flaming tempers to match,' Bryce finished for her. 'Come here, green eyes, I've a lot of catching up to do.'

'I'm not a skinny bird,' Leigh protested as he gathered her to him. 'I'll have you know I've been told I have a model figure.'

'Have you indeed? The poor bloke must have been besotted. Now me, I'm just in love. Have been ever since you scared the daylights out of me when I thought you were going to kill yourself throwing that Tiger Moth around the sky.' And he proceeded to demonstrate just how much in no uncertain terms.

Five minutes later Leigh emerged breathless and trembling. 'Hey, the last man who tried that in a plane offered me money!'

Bryce reluctantly lifted his head from the valley between her breasts and said, 'Our friend Hollander, I presume.'

'Yes. He offered me five hundred pounds, then doubled it, and then told me to name my price. He said that everyone had a price.'

His hand came up to gently twine itself in her hair. 'And have you a price, Leigh?'

Leigh looked at him, her eyes warm and tender. 'Just love.'

His hand stilled and he gazed at her for a long moment before bending to gently kiss her lips. 'Well, I think I can meet your price,' he said lightly, 'but can you meet mine?'

Leigh laughed in surprise. 'What's that?'

'Just—marriage,' he replied smoothly.

She stared at him, wondering for a second if he was serious when she saw the devilment in his eyes. Then she smiled. 'I think I can meet that.'

'Good. So why don't you take over the control of this plane and take us home? We have some unfinished business, remember?'

Leigh smiled into his eyes. 'I remember,' she said softly, and turned the plane to descend through the sunlit sky.

Harlequin® Plus
NOT FOR MEN ONLY!

On a warm spring morning in 1932, an unsuspecting Irish farmer was astonished to see a small airplane fly in from the west and land in his pasture. The farmer was even more surprised when a tall slender woman in aviator clothing stepped from the plane and said, "Hello, I've come from America."

The pilot was Amelia Earhart, an American aviatrix. She had just completed the first solo flight by a woman across the Atlantic Ocean.

Amelia Earhart was born in Kansas in 1898. As a young girl she was completely entranced by airplanes—which at that time had only just been invented. Against the wishes of her family, she learned to fly, and amazed her teachers with a natural ability to master the principles of flight.

After her record-breaking flight across the Atlantic, followed by solo flight from Hawaii to California—again the first by a woman—Amelia became a celebrity. She also became actively involved in the development of commercial aviation in the United States.

But her adventuresome nature demanded challenge. In 1937 she decided to fly around the world at the equator. Tragically, after completing two-thirds of the trip, her plane disappeared somewhere over the South Pacific, and no trace has ever been found.

Not only were Amelia Earhart's accomplishments milestones in the early history of aviation. When President Hoover presented her with the gold medal of the National Geographic Society, she modestly stated, "I shall be happy if my exploit has drawn attention to the fact that women, too, are flying."

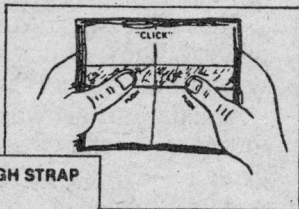

Now's your chance to discover the earlier
books in this exciting series.

Choose from this list of great

SUPERROMANCES!

#8 BELOVED INTRUDER   Jocelyn Griffin

#9 SWEET DAWN OF DESIRE   Meg Hudson

#10 HEART'S FURY   Lucy Lee

#11 LOVE WILD AND FREE   Jocelyn Haley

#12 A TASTE OF EDEN   Abra Taylor

#13 CAPTIVE OF DESIRE   Alexandra Sellers

#14 TREASURE OF THE HEART   Pat Louis

#15 CHERISHED DESTINY   Jo Manning

#16 THIS DARK ENCHANTMENT   Rosalind Carson

#17 CONTRACT FOR MARRIAGE   Megan Alexander

#18 DANCE OF DESIRE   Lisa Lenore

#19 GIVE US FOREVER   Constance F. Peale

#20 JOURNEY INTO LOVE   Jessica Logan

#21 RIVER OF DESIRE   Abra Taylor

#22 MIDNIGHT MAGIC   Christine Hella Cott

#23 FROM THIS BELOVED HOUR   Willa Lambert

#24 CALL OF THE HEART   Wanda Dellamere

#25 INFIDEL OF LOVE   Casey Douglas

SUPERROMANCE

Complete and mail this coupon today!

- -

Worldwide Reader Service

In the U.S.A.
1440 South Priest Drive
Tempe, AZ 85281

In Canada
649 Ontario Street
Stratford, Ontario N5A 6W2

Please send me the following SUPERROMANCES. I am enclosing my check or money order for $2.50 for each copy ordered, plus 75¢ to cover postage and handling.

☐ # 8   ☐ # 14   ☐ # 20
☐ # 9   ☐ # 15   ☐ # 21
☐ # 10   ☐ # 16   ☐ # 22
☐ # 11   ☐ # 17   ☐ # 23
☐ # 12   ☐ # 18   ☐ # 24
☐ # 13   ☐ # 19   ☐ # 25

Number of copies checked @ $2.50 each =	$_____
N.Y. and Ariz. residents add appropriate sales tax	$_____
Postage and handling	$_____ .75
TOTAL	$_____

I enclose_____ .
(Please send check or money order. We cannot be responsible for cash sent through the mail.)
Prices subject to change without notice.

NAME_____
_____(Please Print)_____
ADDRESS_____APT. NO._____
CITY_____
STATE/PROV._____
ZIP/POSTAL CODE_____
Offer expires September 30, 1983

30356000000